Born in Nouméa, New Caledonia in 1886, FRANCIS CARCO arrived in Paris during the winter of his 24th year, in January 1910. Making a beeline for the soon-to-be legendary cabaret, Le Lapin Agile, he was quickly accepted into the inner circle of a Parisian bohemia. There, on La Butte Montmartre, he rubbed shoulders with the likes of Picasso, Modigliani, Utrillo, Max Jacob, Pierre Mac Orlan, Apollinaire, and many of the other leading lights of a Parisian avant-garde. As the author of over 100 books, Carco's talents were plentiful. He composed poetry, literary fiction, plays, memoirs, and biography, and was even known as a witty and engaging *chansonnier*. But with each of these creative expressions his manner remains that of a poet: utilizing a personal vision to unravel and portray the spiritual enigmas that life presents. He was also possessed by a prescient perception and published the first critical essay on Modigliani, whose work he began to collect during a period when other French critics merely scoffed at the contributions of this modern master. Likewise, his early essays on Utrillo, forged by his personal interaction with the painter, exemplify Carco's remarkable insight.

In 1922, Carco was awarded Le Grand Prix du Roman for his novel *L'Homme traqué* ("The Noose of Sin"), and in 1937 he was elected to the Académie Goncourt. During WWII Carco fled to Switzerland with his Jewish wife, Éliane Négrin. Upon returning to France, he was elected to the board of directors of the Comité national des écrivains, the institution that determined which writers were to be blacklisted due to their shameful collaboration with the Nazi regime.

ROB COUTEAU is a Brooklyn-born author and visual artist. His publications have been praised in *Evergreen Review*, *Publishers Weekly*, *New Art Examiner*, *Midwest Book Review*, and *Witty Partition*. In 1985 he won the North American Essay Award, sponsored by the American Humanist Association. His work has been cited in the *New York Times* and in books such as *Ghetto Images in Twentieth-Century American Literature* by Tyrone Simpson, *Gabriel Garcia Marquez's 'Love in the Time of Cholera'* by Thomas Fahy, *Conversations with Ray Bradbury* edited by Steven Aggelis, and David Cohen's *Forgotten Millions*, a book about the homeless. His interviews include conversations with Pulitzer Prize-winning author Justin Kaplan, *Last Exit to Brooklyn* novelist Hubert Selby, Simon & Schuster editor Michael Korda, LSD discoverer Albert Hofmann, Picasso's model and muse Sylvette David, sci-fi author Ray Bradbury, film star and bibliophile Neil Pearson, and historian Philip Willan, author *Puppetmasters: The Political Use of Terrorism in Italy*. Couteau has appeared as a guest on Bob Barrett's *The Best of Our Knowledge* (WAMC), Len Osanic's *Black Op Radio*, and on Monocle 24 in Europe. In 2023 he published *Intimate Souvenirs*, a memoir featuring an Introduction by Robert Roper, author of *Nabokov in America: On the Road to Lolita* and *Now the Drum of War: Walt Whitman and His Brothers in the Civil War*. Since 2020 he has devoted himself to republishing annotated texts of important but forgotten authors such as Stanley Marks, Charles Beadle, and Francis Carco.

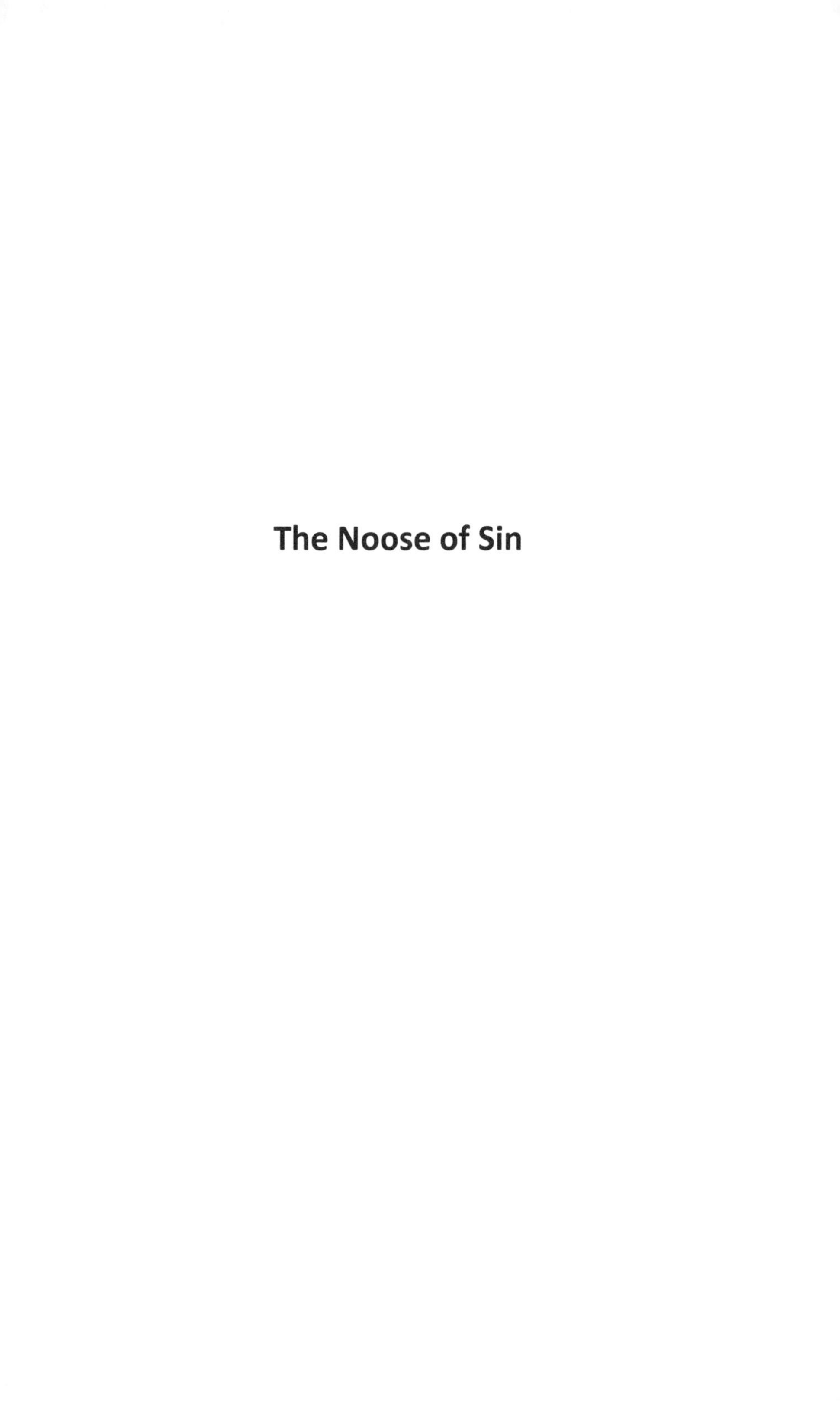

# The Noose of Sin

**Max Jacob's portrait of Francis Carco**

**The Noose of Sin by Francis Carco**

Edited with Annotations and an Afterword
by Rob Couteau

Translated from the French
by Emile Hope

# CONTENTS

*This edition is dedicated
to the lovely Khadija*

Lampieur looked along his shelves. He had arranged the loaves and the croissants he had taken from the oven, in neat rows. There was a hot, heavy smell of fresh bread in the shop, and the dawn struggled in, cold and yellow.

He climbed the staircase slowly, for his night's work was over, but its heaviness still lay upon him like lead. Once in the room overhead, he lay down and slept. Directly he awoke, his uneasy misery of mind awoke with him and drove him again. He pulled on an old pair of slippers and then wrenched open the attic window to let in a waft of fresh air. It was a small window looking out over a world of roofs, and he stood by it listening to the noises that came up to him from the street. He set himself to distinguish these noises very carefully one by one. The thunder of the motor bus that passed along the Rue Rambuteau, the swinging tinkle, distant but perfectly audible, of a bell on the handbarrow of a hawker's cart.

To each of these sounds he listened with the fixed attention of a man who, having lost his way, fastens upon any small detail which may help him to find it again. His sense of security strengthened as he stood there. Very soon he would go down the staircase and become part of it all. The heavy mechanical vibrations, the lights in distant windows, conveyed reality and protection to his mind.

Yet Lampieur did not hurry himself. A fancy leapt upon him that someone was waiting for him on the further side of the closed door. All his passing sense of comfort dissolved again, though he knew that the passage leading to the staircase was empty. There was no one outside to bar his way.

Making a final effort he left the room. He glanced backwards more than once as he went, until he gained the street, where he was lost in the crowd.

# CHAPTER 1

For three weeks the police had been searching for the man who had committed a murder in the Rue Saint-Denis, and every night of those weeks Lampieur had gone regularly to a little cabaret near the market. He was very well known there, and the patron always greeted him with great friendliness.

"Here you are, Monsieur François, always [on] time," he said as he poured out two glasses of white Bordeaux; and putting them on the zinc counter, he swallowed one down himself to his customer's very good health.

It was the dead hour of the day. Only a few shabby clients sat on the benches along the walls, smoking ends of cigarettes which they had gathered up in the streets, or reading old newspapers as they sat over plates of half-eaten food. Near the entrance a woman, who was known as "Everybody's Mother," stared dully into the dirty street, lying in wait for fresh arrivals to ask for alms with a certain touch of dignity.

The cabaret, for all its dirt and the strong smell of humanity, was not without character of a kind. Every-one who went there was or had been unlucky. Hatless prostitutes with slovenly clothes and dirty hands trooped in at night, to warm themselves by the stove. Renée with a bad abscess on her neck, Madame Berthe grasping her umbrella in case anyone should steal it from her, Gilberte who was far gone in consumption, fat Thérèse Yvette, Gaby, Lilas who came from

Brittany, and Léontine who had run away from home because she wanted to see life.

Lampieur knew most of the women who went there, as he passed them every day in the neighborhood of the blind old house where he worked. Sometimes he said "Good night" to them and went on, past the rows of shuttered shops, without troubling himself further about them.

At midnight they were all still in the streets, and five or six of them usually came back very late to the Rue Saint-Denis, passing the air hole of the baker's shop to call to him for a loaf of fresh bread. He had hung a piece of string outside which could be let down to him, as they threw him their coppers, and the string was then put back in its place for the next who came, to lower it in her turn for a hot loaf.

Lampieur hated these women with their shrill voices that called to him from outside. The very fact of their being in the street at a time when no one else was about except a stray policeman, solitary foot passengers, drunken men getting home as best they could, and those strange shadowy figures who hardly seem real at all, outraged something in his nature.

They disturbed him at his work, calling and screaming at him.

"All right, all right," he shouted back angrily. "Don't make such a filthy noise."

All this maddening irritation for the sake of twopence-worth of bread. He was not obliged to let them have it. What were they at now, instead of pulling up the string?

"Good God!" he shouted, "pull it up."

He could never look at the dangling string which seemed to hang from nowhere at all, without a feeling of horror, never, since the night he came back to his bakery and saw it swaying in the draught. . . . Who had let it down to him and asked for bread while he was away? He hardly dared even to ask himself the question. He had stood there gaping at it stupidly, unable to pull himself together.

At last he caught hold of it, and tying it round a loaf threw it upwards into the street above. Then, someone had come without saying a word and taken the bread.


"What a night," Madame Berthe said, shaking her wet umbrella as she came to the stove where Gilberte was coughing softly.

"Have a gin?" Fat Thérèse suggested.

"I will." Gilberte's voice was husky and thick.

"And the rest of you?" Léontine asked the others.

Lampieur, who was leaning against the zinc counter, watched them as they drank. All his silent misery was caused by one of those women, and he could not tell which. Whichever of them it was, she knew that he had been away from the bakery the night of the crime, just at the very time that was mentioned in all the papers the following day. He wondered if any of them were watching him suspiciously.

During these first days he believed himself absolutely lost, and a mad desire to go away at once drove him almost over the edge of self-betrayal. But some invisible force held him where he was, close to the very spot where the drama had been played out.

Not that he was fascinated and drawn against his will to look at the entrance to the house. The long ugly hall with its dull dirty tiles, and the door he had gone through, leading into the concierge's room. . . . He would have walked miles sooner than pass that place again. The reason was infinitely more secret and subtle, so that he could not analyze it or even understand. He only kept away from the house, but otherwise he lived exactly the same life as before, day after day.

"I'll have a grog," Léontine spoke loudly.

"That makes three."

She was not much more than a child, but was one of the products of all towns, faded, without ever having had any real color, looking thirty years old at twenty, and never very much older later on. Small, and badly made, she had a suggestion of something different to the rest, and even her way of talking was quieter and less provocative.

Lampieur watched her eyes. Did she know? He could not tell as he took careful note of her, showing nothing of the awful anxiety he felt. He noticed every gesture she made, her quick glances to left and right, he soft and rather sad blue of her eyes, and the submissive way she spoke to Lilas, the Breton girl, and Yvette whose black hair was gathered into a net.

"Which of them?" Lampieur asked himself.

He was defeated by his own question, and yet it was hopeless to think he might surprise anything out of them. He would have given anything he possessed to know in whose power he lay so completely that she had only to open her lips to hand him over body and soul to the police.

Would she speak? Why hadn't she spoken already? What had kept her silent? Lampieur could not guess. But to keep silence as she was doing made her, at any rate, his accomplice, and through that fact he had her at his mercy.

## CHAPTER 2

He lived in perpetual uncertainty, haunted, tormented, driven by moods and fancies, and yet his crime, the thing he had done, never once obsessed him. He hardly ever remembered how he had smothered the old woman in the dark little room and stolen her money. Not a gleam of remorse overtook him. He congratulated himself, and felt he had done very well when he hid the money he had taken behind the plaster of the big oven, covering the hole he had made so that no one could possibly discover it. No one ever came there, no one would guess, and it gave him a place of quiet in the very nerve centre of his racking anxiety.

He had carried it all through alone, and yet by this one wretched oversight on his part, someone, still hidden behind a thin veil of mystery, might come forward and claim the price of silence. At times he thought of going straight to the police station and pointing out to them the coincidence of his being absent from the bakery at the very hour of the murder. That would be better than letting someone else go there instead.

"Just a perfectly simple coincidence," he could say.

But then there would be the further necessity of keeping the police off his track. Lampieur's courage failed at the thought. That further necessity would entail evidence which pointed towards the truth. Evidence and witnesses. There was the little servant who, three months before the crime, had heard the concierge talk of the quarter's rent paid by the tenants which she carried in her dress.

Another woman who went there to wash the passages had talked of it and said that she was foolish to boast as she had, and the owner of the house warned her more than once.

"Hide your employer's money, Madame Courte," she advised her.

"If I had anywhere to hide it," the old fool had said.

As he put his loaves along the shelves in his shop he remembered the cold light of the gray winter morning when, without thinking very seriously of it, the knowledge that Madame Courte had nearly three thousand francs in her shabby old purse, filled him with a kind of dull wonder.

He could think of no answer to the questions he might be faced with at any moment, but though he often sank into despair he buoyed himself up again. Who should suspect him? His life was a perfectly open and honest one, his whole conduct called for no criticism. People spoke well of him. He never drank or had bouts of dissipation like most of the workmen in the quarter, and he even avoided the more respectable dancing rooms. As for the cabaret near the markets where he went every evening of his life to drink his glass of white Bordeaux, he had been going there for years, and Fouasse could swear to the fact that in all that time he had never once seen him drunk.

Silent and steady-going, with his cropped head and his trousers caught at the waist with a leather belt, his decent blue socks and his slightly bent shoulders, he looked what he was, a man of about forty, heavy and dull but honest and dependable. He talked very little and listened to the others who complained at the shortage of "fags," of what they had done, of the police. No one heeded him at all until he put down his glass on the counter and said "The same."

His habitual reserve made it easy for Lampieur to keep his slow silence when the man who had been reading the paper asked Monsieur Fouasse his views on the subject of the murder.

"And you'll see, Monsieur Francois," the patron of the cabaret said, "that they won't catch that lascar."[1]

"Ah," Lampieur nodded.

"They will not. What will you bet?"

Lampieur never made any bets. He raised his head, and with a hand that shook a little swallowed his drink at one gulp.

"They'll never catch him," the patron said again to the company. "First of all because, to carry out such a murder in the most crowded street in the market, the man can be no fool. My idea is that he wasn't the only one. Someone helped him, or anyhow, a woman kept guard while he did the work."

"A woman?"

Monsieur Fouasse shrugged his shoulders.

"I think so," he said conclusively. "And if they catch him out, it will be she who has sold him, as usual."

"As usual," Lampieur echoed, and draining the dregs of his glass he went out with his heavy step, his

---

[1] Lascar: an Indian sailor, army servant, or artilleryman. From Hindi and Urdu: *lashka*, army.

mind dark with a sick feeling of dread, not daring to search further to find the woman to whom he felt himself to be bound, henceforward.

Yet he was only back in the bakery, and alone in front of the oven, the kneading trough and the pans for the bread piled one on the other in a corner, when the thought of the girl came back to torture him. At first the idea of her had given him the feeling that she was perpetually getting up from the corner and coming to meet him, but now she remained there silently, without ever stirring from her place. She was waiting for something.

He collected himself and threw off his fear, and rolling the dough out on the board, he shook a light handful of dry flour over it. When that was done, he walked backwards and forwards to the oven, making up the fire and driving out the thought that lay, shadowy, in his brain. His watch hung on a nail on the wall, showing him the time as he molded the dough and made it into shape. He thought of nothing at all. The oven was heating well, and in the underground room the man at the board forgot his misery of mind, looking up at the watch now and then as the hands slowly moved, marking the passing of the night.

Subconsciously Lampieur was a prey to anxiety which made him listen to the lightest sound. She always returned. She drew him towards her, and if he struggled against her dangerous magnetism he lost hold of himself. To intensify his nervous terrors she became one with the smallest rustle behind him in the cellar or the most distant echo along the street. Every passing footstep on the pavement was hers.

From the bakery, Lampieur could see nothing, and he did not dare to go up into the street, or even stand for long by the air hole. What Fouasse had said in the cabaret came back to his mind. It was always a woman who sold the pass. A woman went by the shop at that moment. What was she thinking about? Why was she walking up and down overhead, and not going onwards, away from him? What did she want there? Did she intend to haunt him night after night and force him to come out and betray himself? He knew that if he ever gave way to the impulse he was a lost man. Not if he left his work to go up—and look at the girl, but because he would inevitably speak to her and ask her why she suspected him.

Already in the cabaret where the women had gathered round the stove, he sometimes imagined it to be one of them, and sometimes another. He swore to himself that he would never speak to any of them, and so far he had conquered his longing to do so. What could he say, in any case? It was only a mad impulse, one of those unguarded flashes of folly that carry a man straight to disaster. Lampieur had foreseen all this and resisted the temptation, but he knew his own danger each time he played with the longing. He began to wonder if he was going mad, or whether it was all a dream. Something one could awaken from and know it had never happened.

There were nights when he was possessed by an extraordinarily clear impression of his hidden accomplice. He imagined her going away and coming back to the air hole. The night of the murder she must have been prowling like a cat in the dark. At first she had probably been surprised to see no one in the bakery, and then she was sure to have become curious. She must have called to him in her shrill voice, knelt down and peered in. Thrown him her coppers and the string, and looked again to see whether he was asleep. How long had she waited? In the end, she had gone away. Had she come back before he returned to the cellar? If she had repeated the maneuver several times, or shouted to make herself heard, a passerby or a neighbor might have easily stopped to find out what was up, and afterwards, several days later, gone to the police station and given secret information against him.

All this was quite likely. The girl who now waited and loitered up and down in front of his shop was probably there under police orders. If so, her reason was clear as day. She was the trap. Sooner or later Lampieur would come into the street, and faced by her, he was morally certain to give himself away. He wasn't the type of man to face that kind of situation with any courage or success.

He would deny that he had been out at the hour when the murder had been committed.

Who had seen him? He was asleep behind the pile of logs by the oven. Anyone can go to sleep, there is no law against that. If your job is to work when other people are in bed, you do get tired. Plenty of bakeries had to give up their night shifts as the men wouldn't do the work for them. Let them prove that he was not asleep in his cellar. That was his defense. He would stick to that all through.

Yet why should he wear himself out over this nagging question of defense? No one had accused him of anything.

A sudden idea came to him that he would leave the cellar and go to the cabaret and have a drink, so as to establish a kind of belated alibi.

There was no one in the street. Lampieur could hardly believe his eyes. He could have sworn she was there, as she had been every other night.

The empty street stretched away with its dim reflections of lamplight, its echoes and its closed shop fronts. Further off, the outline of the market stood up huge and dark, and already sounds of life came from there, and carts began to pass him in the road.

## CHAPTER 3

The days and nights went on in their dull incoherence, and Lampieur, who counted them carefully, could not understand the sick misery they brought. He had to drag through them somehow. February was nearly over, Paris was deep in slush and mire, and everything was sodden and dirty. Rain shut in the streets, and people who walked along the pavement turned into a dreary procession of umbrellas, cold and depressing to watch.

Lampieur got up late. He was down by six o'clock with nothing to do. The market was empty at that hour, and the broken pavement reflected the lights from inside. A marshy smell hung about the place, icy and sour, and filtered along the neighboring streets, where the refuse of the day lay in the gutter, adding to the heavy odor of decay.

In the cabaret belonging to Fouasse the atmosphere was thick and stifling. It did not affect Lampieur, who was well used to it; he even breathed it in with a sense of satisfaction, like a man who has awakened after a nightmare and comes back to the realities of life, thankful to find that it was only a dream.

Each time he went to the cabaret, Léontine was there. She either came in after he had arrived, or left before he did, and whenever he met her look, he found it more and more difficult to hide his suspicions of her. Why was she always there? She seemed changed, somehow, and was not with the other women any more; she went about alone. Her eyes were larger, they seemed to eat up her pinched face, and she had a dragged, helpless look. He noticed that specially. These constant meetings could not account for it, he told himself, and he wondered whether she wanted to speak to him. What had she in her mind? If there really was something she wished to say, why did she seem so driven and unnatural? He knew that he was afraid of her, and as it grew towards the time when he had to go back to work, his fear intensified, and left him without strength to fight it off.

The thought of her began to take a more positive form in his mind and made him more and more restless. Her eyes haunted him, and he brooded over her walk, her little personal tricks of manner. The obstinate gentleness, the wondering sadness of her look. She stood before him so clearly that he felt he had only to hold out his hands to touch her. He heard someone walking overhead, and recognized her footsteps.

"What does it mean?" he asked wildly.

He tried to collect himself and face this shadowy terror which followed him so softly, but his courage failed. He was drenched in sweat, and he wondered if he called out to her whether she would reply. Certainly she was there by the air hole. No one else had the same walk. A morbid craving made her come back to pace up and down the street, and hang about the bakery—like a lost soul. She was there for hours and hours without moving from the place. Was she waiting for him to call out to her? There was nothing to prevent his doing that if he wanted to. No risk of any kind. If he shouted up at her, what matter? He need not even call her by name. A whistle, a word or two, asking who it was. . . . She would understand all right. After a minute she would lean over and look down, and he could say, "What the devil do you want?"

Arguing with himself in this way, Lampieur avoided the air hole, but the idea of calling Léontine had worked his mind into a state of panic. He walked up and down the cellar, and it was some time before he was calm enough to go back to his work. He had been like a man who narrowly escapes drowning, and catches at a straw to save himself. All the past swept over him again. He was clinging to his slender hope of life which might give way at any moment. He groped at the idea of Léontine with shaking hands, because a worse terror had presented itself to him. Somewhere inside his brain a voice said to him that Léontine was not up there in the street. It was someone else, perhaps there was no one out at all, and the voice kept on and on telling him to go up and see for himself. That there never had been anyone there, those nights when he had gone out to look along the street. It was the sound of the rain he had heard, the rain and the wind. "Go up and look," the voice repeated again and again.

Lampieur held out against it. The shadow of his awful misgiving flickered along the walls of the cellar, and he watched it steadily. It leapt and fell, clung to the corners and slid towards the air hole, trying to escape. The voice was silent, but in the silence he fancied a thousand echoes which he could not hear and yet which tingled and rang along the nerves of his whole body.

He set himself with ferocious obstinacy against the desire to go up into the street. There was no one there. He would not go, no, he would not go. It was torture, but the sense of having conquered himself gave him a touch of desperate triumph.

It was only a lull in the fight. Each time the obsession came back to him Lampieur lost ground, and each spell of calm was invaded by a more fierce attack, followed by a deadness that lay at the mercy of the steady dropping that wears out a stone. His will evaporated.

What was he waiting for?

Lampieur knew the answer to that question only too well. Somewhere in some night there lay a fatal hour for him, when he would break under this driving power which was too strong to resist. He would go up into the street and see who it really was.

## CHAPTER 4

Léontine was in the street.

From behind the shutters in the shop, Lampieur had watched her pass, and he waited, keeping perfectly quiet until she came back in her noiseless way, the same way in which she had already passed.

She did not know that he watched her. Her clothes were drenched and her shoes broken, but she hardly noticed anything. She was obviously under the power of some absorbing idea that sent her walking towards him so quietly. Lampieur, who was watching for her to turn, realized that he could not hear her coming.

This struck him as very strange. How was it, that down in the cellar he had recognized her step, when she really moved onwards like a shadow? . . . She had startled him; so little was he prepared for this when he had first seen her slip past into the darkness beyond. How far was she going to walk down the street, before she returned? He did not know. He could imagine a dozen reasons as he held his breath and stood hidden behind the shutters, fearing to let her know that he was there, watching.

She was taking a long time to come back, and the shutters prevented his seeing more than a short stretch of pavement exactly opposite to him. She might be waiting beyond where he could see. The noise of carts going to the market, with the hooting of heavy motor horns came to his ears, and the wind blew a cold splash of rain between the crevices of the shutters. There was nothing else. Nothing was stirring, except the wind and the lash of the rain tearing down the sleeping street.

Little by little, Lampieur lost hold of himself. A fear born out of his desire to see her come back made him forget the careful reasoning which had brought him there.

The expression Fouasse had used drove him. "If they catch him out," he said, "a woman will have sold him, as usual." Lampieur repeated the sentence stupidly. Each word, each letter was printed on his mind. He had given way to the ghastly curiosity he had felt, to find out who it was who walked in front of his shop. Would he have the strength to prevent himself from following that woman and letting her guess the torture he suffered? He could not be sure.

If he changed her suspicion of him to a certainty, if he gave himself away, Fouasse, without knowing it, had warned him in advance.

"If they catch him out." Lampieur spelled it slowly as though reading it in print.

*"If they catch him out."*

There was a great deal in that one short sentence. Something brutal…. "If they caught Lampieur out." Exactly, and why not? He had not forgotten the murder, he simply never thought of it. It wasn't the crime, it was the piece of string that complicated everything. Murderers were said to suffer from remorse. He was a murderer, but he had no feeling of the kind; he did not know what it meant. At the end of the first few days he had been astonished as well as frightened. After that fear had driven out everything else, so that he did not trouble his mind about the murder so long as he could go on living as he had, before it was committed. He appeared to have made a compact between his conscience and his ordinary routine of life, and then, as there was nothing to fear from that quarter, Lampieur was forced to think and continue to think of his accomplice who could denounce him, and the one thing which mattered was, to escape from her.

"If they catch him out," he said aloud, "catch him out." The thought was unbearable. There was something mocking and cynical about it. Something that warned him to look out for himself, and yet would not give any help. This girl was the woman Fouasse had spoken of, his worst enemy on earth. He knew that. The heavy horror of mind began to overcome him again, and he relaxed before it with a kind of morbid satisfaction in letting himself go.

If Léontine had returned at that moment nothing would have prevented Lampieur from telling the whole story.

He had opened the door of the shop, so as to see the length of the street, but Léontine was not there. An anger against her seized him. She had straggled off into a bar to drink, or was wandering about the lighted booths in the market, watching the vegetable carts come in. He imagined her there, white and shadowy in the crowd, looking about without really seeing anything. A touch of something that was almost jealousy stung him, bitter, evil, and yet charged with a kind of dull vividness. Since he had seen Léontine and become sure that it was she who prowled around the bakery by night, he felt that she belonged to him. Without attempting to analyze his feeling about her, he knew only that if it had not been for the strange attraction the knowledge of his secret exercised on her mind, his sense of possession would not have existed. He saw that quite distinctly.

Why had she not come back? Why had she shown none of her usual obstinate determination to hang about round his shop? Why?

He went outside the door. The night wind dulled him, and the rain was driven into his face. Close to the air hole Léontine was standing perfectly still. He saw her flat against the wall like a shadow,—he dared not venture to approach.

"Who is it?" he said, keeping at a distance. "Who is it? What do you want here?"

The shadowy figure made no reply.

"Are you deaf?" Lampieur shouted. "I'm speaking to you. Can't you hear me?"

He thought she seemed about to run away.

"Why do you hang about here every night?" He hurried on and stood full in her path, and repeated "Every night?" He was beside her, but the movement he made to prevent her passing him was hardly visible.

"I suppose you don't come deliberately to annoy me?" he asked again after a short silence. "Can't you answer? Perhaps you only want to be a worry to me. I know you well enough. You've got to explain this before I let you go."

He came a little closer to her, opening and shutting his hands and breathing hard.

"No, don't." Léontine raised her arm.

Lampieur gave a rough laugh, and thrusting his hands into his pockets, waited, standing before her. Léontine said nothing. She seemed to fix her eyes on some vague, terrifying point of distance as she shivered, crouching and bent against the wall.

"Well?" he asked.

He was surprised at his own self-control in not having taken her and shaken a reply from her. But how long did she intend to stay like this? He looked at her with heavy scrutiny, and was no longer afraid of her. A sense of emptiness, a queer, inward void which it made him giddy to look down into, came instead. He recalled himself to her, and the impression of the abyss weighed more heavily upon him. It prevented him from moving towards her and paralyzed him afresh, sending a shudder through him.

"You won't answer?" he asked.

His hands, deep in his pockets, felt as heavy as lead, and he could not move them. He could not catch Léontine and hold her; not that it mattered, for she was terrified of him already. Her teeth were chattering, her whole body shook, and now and then she raised her head with an effort.

"There!" he said. "Don't be frightened. Am I likely to do you any harm?" She seemed to try to answer. "I," Lampieur went on violently, "I don't want to hurt you. It's not true. It wasn't me . . ." He said it over again, though his voice was hardly intelligible. "I tell you it wasn't me."

Once it had been said, he experienced a feeling of relief, though he had not explained anything in saying it. She looked at him at last, caught at him and held frantically to his arm, bursting into a flood of tears.

## CHAPTER 5

Lampieur never forgot the warmth and almost sensual pleasure he felt in listening to her sobbing. She was different from that moment, less a woman to him than an ally, and he was sorry for her.

"Why are you crying?" he asked.

She lay on his arm as heavy as lead, and he held her up, dragging her along. She was drenched to the skin and he could not leave her there in the rain. A feeling of pity lightened up his misery.

"You mustn't cry like that, it's no use," he repeated.

She let him carry her, all her strength had gone and she could not have walked a step alone, without falling. He had kept his arm round her, and she realized that he was taking her to the bakery.

"Come along," he repeated, pushing open the door, and seating her on a chair.

She had stopped crying, but the shivering fits still shook her and prevented her thinking clearly. All she knew was, that she was no longer outside in the rain. It was warm and quiet. In the half-light which came up the staircase from the cellar below she could see the outline of the counter, the shelves where Lampieur put the bread, and a scales for weighing it.

She called to him.

"Here I am," he said, shrugging up his shoulders.

With an effort she drove back the fancies which haunted her mind and danced before her eyes. She saw the whirlpool towards which she was being swept, the power which, ever since the night of the murder, had dragged her back to the air hole where

Lampieur had found her. Now she was close to the object of so much suspense, and was no longer in the street. There was nothing to prevent her from following the line of lamplight which made a fantastic pathway to the staircase, and going down into the cellar....

"Where are you going?" Lampieur shouted after her, but she did not turn her head. She could see the first steps of the staircase, the rope that served for a banister, and the vaulted roof of the basement. The light from below struck upwards on to her face and eyes, and Lampieur realized that he could not stop her.

"Hold on to the rope and stoop your head," he said, directing her.

She did as he told her obediently, and went downwards with the stiff movements of a marionette. He bent suddenly forward, staring down into the cellar, with an idea which he knew to be half insane seizing him suddenly. He had wondered whether he had left any evidence of the murder lying about down there. There was nothing to leave, so he must be mad. He looked at the walls, the earth floor, the rolling board covered with a piece of oilcloth, the pile of logs and his old slippers; a tablecloth and some baskets on a rickety old table at which he sat about midnight to eat some bread and cheese. One by one he examined them all, and everything was in its place. There was no reason why they should not have been. No one had been there, no one looked after the place except himself, and yet he looked at them distrustfully as though they had it in their power to betray him to Léontine.

The girl stood in the centre of the room. Her suspense began to lessen its tension though her mind was in utter confusion, and her thoughts still danced fantastically. She was in a cellar. There was the rolling board, the stove, the opening of the air hole, and quite close to her, the man who was in the bakery when she came to buy bread. She had never pictured Lampieur as being there, and his presence upset everything for her again. It made it impossible to recall things clearly and to recapture in all its horror the fresh sense of discovery of the empty cellar. Except for the fact that she had now come into it herself, it was just as she had seen it when she threw down her coppers the night of murder.

"Sit down," Lampieur said, leaning on the table. "Nearer the fire. That's better. It's warm there, and you are less in the way while I work."

"Yes, oh yes," she answered him dully.

She sat down and watched him pile the logs in the stove and then pull off his coat and sweater, and take out a few loaves on a tin.

"They're baked," he said after a moment.

She nodded silently.

A warm heavy smell filled the air pleasantly, the smell of burning wood and bread, and she drew it in with a deep breath.

"It's queer," she said. "It reminds me of when I was little and used to go out on errands. . . ."

"Ah," he said, without attending to her.

He came back to the fire. Somewhere at a distance a clock sounded two faint strokes in the night.

"Didn't the others go with you on errands?" he asked.

"Which others?"

"To fetch the bread?" he said, speaking in a low voice.

She looked up at the air hole. "Why do you wait for them?" she asked.

"I?" Turning his head, he looked at her. "I don't wait for them. They come along. Sometimes I am here, and they don't always come." He spoke slowly, as though he was unwilling to say so much. You don't believe me?"

She gave no answer. Why should he say that, she asked him at last.

"All right, all right," he grumbled at her, going back to his work. "Only ..." He did not finish the sentence, and a heavy silence fell between him and Léontine.

## CHAPTER 6

The next day he found Léontine at the cabaret at the usual time, and the impression she made on his mind was different to what he expected. He was almost glad to see her there, it came as a relief. In any case, she meant nothing to him as an individual, though indirectly she mattered a great deal. He was perfectly quiet now, and had been all through the day. Whether she knew this or not, he couldn't tell, but he was sure of himself again, and had nothing to be afraid of.

From where she sat, Léontine watched him, and was there because he was there. It increased his sense of power over her, — he had secretly hoped to find her at the cabaret. There would be no more return to the torments and agony of his mind, and his heart lightened as at the lifting of an intolerable weight. For the first time since the night of the murder, things looked real and natural again. Chaos had been transformed into a reasonable orderly world. It was like a miracle.

Around him were the usual crowd of shivering ill-clad men and women, the girls off the streets, drunkards, and all the ragbag clientele Fouasse served. Some of them sat by tables and others leaned on the zinc counter, but not one of them took any notice of Lampieur. They were, in fact, the usual lamentable group of waifs and vagabonds who were washed up, so to speak, out of the markets, and might be found in any drinking place in the neighborhood, trying to keep out the cold of the night. Lampieur was so used to them that he took them all for granted, and yet once he had actually feared them. He cared less than nothing for them now.

As for the women, the remark Fouasse had made remained in his memory, but it did not affect him as it had. He had stripped the affair of its mystery, so that it menaced him no longer. What could Léontine do, after all? She knew nothing for certain, she could say nothing. He had held back his desire to speak, and had dominated her. Then she had left, and he had gone with her as far as the door of the shop and no one had seen them together.

"Well?" asked Monsieur Fouasse, as they shook hands over the counter and the patron invited him to have a drink.

Out in the street the lights fell crossways, and silhouettes of the passersby were thrown on the window of the bar for a moment as they went onwards. A mist dimmed the glass, traced by long lines of water where the drops trickled slowly down. The same wet fog dulled the one mirror of the establishment, in its brown frame. On the floor amid the cigarette ends and sawdust, little streams traced their way, and whenever the door opened an icy wind swept in, bearing on it the confused sounds of the street outside.

"Shut the door," two or three men shouted to "Everybody's Mother," who had kept one of her clients on the threshold for a moment. Lampieur shivered.

"Will you shut that door," Fouasse said authoritatively. "I should like to add that I have had to say this twice over."

The night before, Lampieur would hardly have noticed that "Everybody's Mother" had been immediately obedient to the voice of Monsieur Fouasse, but, now, everything interested him down to the smallest details, even though he took no part in what went on.

"That is better," Monsieur said cheerfully.

"That's much better," Lampieur laughed. "Everybody's Mother" had no right to upset people. "No right," he thought, meaning by that, that the weaker must give way. It was the only sensible arrangement. What would have happened if Léontine had wanted to resist? Luckily for her she had not. She effaced herself and kept very quiet sitting over a small glass of wine which she did not drink. . . . He would have no more bother with her. What she thought, her suspicions of him, her uneasy eyes, all that had ceased to count for anything. Even if she attempted to go further in her desire to make perfectly certain, or to gratify her morbid curiosity, he was determined to give her no further clue of any kind. Her wish to know more than she had any right to know, could only complicate things for her, and put her outside their mutual limits. What would happen then? . . . Lampieur suddenly remembered something horrible.

"Well . . ." he said, fumbling in his pocket for a handful of coppers to settle his score with Fouasse. He was thinking that nothing was ever really going to be the same as before. "Good night, Patron."

"So long," Fouasse said in his friendly way.

Outside the cabaret, Lampieur turned the corner into the Rue des Prêcheurs. The air smelt of shellfish and seaweed, and he stood for a minute, thinking of his late sense of security.

"All that was lies . . . he said.

## CHAPTER 7

Lies.

He wanted to get away from them all, those people in there, but Léontine had slipped out of the bar and followed him without his having noticed her. When he went into the restaurant where he had his evening meal, she waited like a dog outside, so that when he came out he nearly stumbled over her in the dark.

His first feeling was one of dismay to find her there, and he started back violently. He was angry with her, but he looked around to collect himself again, the shop lights and the passing taxicabs and carts forming themselves into a moving arabesque of shadows and waving reflections.

"Who set you on to spy on me?" he asked, pulling his cap down over his eyes.

"l am not spying." Her voice was pathetic and a little shrill.

Lampieur looked up and down the road, and along the street, shrugging his heavy shoulders, as she came closer to him.

"Go to hell," he said roughly. "I don't want you. I don't know anything about you. . . ." They stared at one another silently. "For God's sake give me some peace." He turned onwards, slouching along, his hands in his pockets.

She followed him without any protest as far as the bakery. There was no way by which Lampieur could prevent her from doing this. What was there he could do? Whenever he turned round, she was stealing along, just within sight, always watching and watching to see if he looked back at her. At last he stood still and waited. What did the girl want of him? To have her there like his own shadow was nauseating, and he hated her for it.

The passersby in the street drifted along indistinctly, and some women standing in the lamplit door of an unclean, shabby-looking hotel called to him. He turned his back to them and looked up at the outline of the roofs, dark against the sky, towered over by the twin arrows of the Church of Saint Leu.[2]

As soon as she came within speaking distance, he spoke to her. "What do you mean by following me? Is there anything you want to say?"

She nodded her head in silence.

"Be careful," he said in an undertone.

She glanced towards two policemen sheltering in the porch of a house a little further up the hill. "I see them," she said, and her voice was breathless.

They walked on and passed the policemen.

"Last night—" she began.

"What?"

"It was you who came after me."

"I'm not talking of last night," Lampieur said sharply, "I'm talking of now. Why are you after me like this? You do it to annoy me, to give me a lot of worry. I know that much."

"It's something I can't help," she said. "It's not my own fault. Every night and all day it goes on." She put her hand to her breast. "Inside me. I can't help it. It's

---

[2] The Église Saint-Leu-Saint-Gilles de Paris, a Roman Catholic church located in *le 1er arrondissement* of Paris.

not my fault. When you shouted to me not to follow you, it didn't make any difference."

Lampieur raised his arms and let them fall heavily.

"I don't want to follow you." She moved jerkily. "I have to. It's not my fault."

He said nothing, but pulled at the peak of his cap.

"I didn't think any harm the night I came for my loaf," she went on. "I threw down the string and the coppers. . . ."

"That's it," he assented heavily. "I know." He looked about him again at the people and the houses and made an effort to recapture his confidence. "That was the night I fell asleep behind the pile of logs by the stove. I heard someone making a row. . . ."

"I called to you."

"And then you came back later?"

"Yes, I did. I came back several times, and each time I shouted down to you."

Lampieur had been smiling a little, but the smile grew rigid on his face, and his eyes questioned her anxiously.

"You must have seen me the last time you came back," he said. "Weren't there people about?"

"I was alone."

"And when you shouted to me?"

"No one else was there. Only, the next day in the paper there was . . . every one was talking about it. . ."

"What do I care for the papers?" he said savagely. "What does all that prove?" He gave a laugh. "I never even read the papers. Haven't the time. They may print what they like. I'm a working man and have my work to do."

"Don't be angry with me," she said in a frightened voice.

He swung round and looked down at her.

"Give me your arm, quickly," Léontine said, beseeching him.

The police were forming a cordon across the angle of two streets to capture their miserable prey. They appeared from every side in a chain that was lost in the darkness.

"If only I can get through," she said, panting with fright. "Oh, if only I can get through."

"It will be all right," he said, taking her arm and walking towards the cordon where he stood and spoke to a policeman, handing him his identity card. The policeman put his whistle to his lips and blew a shrill call, making an opening for him to pass through with the girl.

"We'd best hurry," Lampieur said, looking round again. "They'll probably close the next street."

"I wouldn't like to have their job," she said, still shaking like a leaf.

They hurried on again through the Rue Tiquetonne, up the black passage of the Grand-Cerf,[3] and neither of them spoke. The passage led into new streets, quieter and darker, and Lampieur and the girl went on together, not quite sure of where they were, but they did not dare to risk going back. There was nothing for it but to go into a small bistro and order a drink, and as they sat down at a round table, Lampieur took out his watch.

---

[3] Rue Tiquetonne is in the *2ème arrondissement*, near the Passage du Grand-Cerf.

"They've done this a dozen times this month," Léontine said.

"And never caught you yet?"

"Never."

"The twelfth police drive," he said as he made a note of the time.

"What are they after?"

"I don't know." He lowered his voice a little. "Sometimes they get hold of someone, to make them talk."

"Is that it?"

"It might be that." Lampieur bent towards her. She was trembling. "Listen," he said in a voice of warning. "It's not a police drive. What do they get out of that, do you suppose? All that trouble for so much rubbish. If they'd caught you . . . yes, you . . . that could easily have happened. . . ."

"I didn't say it couldn't."

"Well, if they did," he labored the point obstinately. "If you had been caught, what would you do?"

"What would I do?" She stared at him without understanding.

"They'd question you. Can't you understand? They'd ask you questions."

"If they did?" she asked.

"If they did. . . . Why nothing. They'd want to know what you'd been up to, why you are always on the prowl round the bakery. Do you suppose they don't know that?"

She listened with painful attention.

"Then, what about this idea of yours, what you told me. That you always want to come back there. Oh, I'm not stone blind."

"I've never talked. . . . I wouldn't," she defended herself weakly.

"I don't trust you. When a woman gets an idea into her head, it's always the same thing in the end." He drew back from her. "I'll say no more about it. That's the best way."

He tilted his chair back, pretending that he was no longer the least interested in the conversation, but his eyes betrayed him horribly, and he kept looking at Léontine.

"That's it," he said in grumbling tones. "We'll say no more about it. You and your ideas. . . . Only," — he stopped, tilting his chair, —"you'll make me angry one of these days, and then I'll stop it."

"Hush, hush!" She put up her hand. "Don't shout at me."

He put his large hand flat on the table and stared into her face. "I will," he said slowly. "As sure as I sit here. I swear it."

The wine they had drunk warmed them a little and called a faint color to their cheeks. Lampieur filled her with loathing even when he attracted her. She had not the least doubt now that he had committed the murder. His ways, his sudden bursts of violence, his suspicions, all accused him. He couldn't keep from talking of it, and wanting to know what she thought. If his conscience was clear, he wouldn't bother his head about any of it.

"What are you thinking of now?" he asked. "Your ideas, I suppose."

"That's it," she said dully.

He moved his hands over the oilcloth on the table, and with a sudden desire to escape, she got up quickly.

"You want to leave," he said. "All right. I've got to get back to work." He drained his glass, drew the back of his hand across his mouth, and paying the sodden, sleepy-looking garçon he followed her out.

He called to her directly they got into the street, and her only reply was a faint drawing in of her breath, but he had to call to her again before she stopped. When he overtook her, they went on together, silently, and with a kind of dumb wretchedness over both of them.

"Not so fast," he said abruptly.

She wavered and stood still. "Don't frighten me again," she said pleadingly. "I'm afraid of you. Is it what I know that makes you angry?" She flung out her arms to him, and tried to cling to him.

"Stop playacting," he said, unclasping her thin arms. "Stop that. You thought I'd done it. Isn't that so?"

"I didn't think anything—"

"About that old woman?" His voice was perfectly flat. "Here, don't be frightened of me."

She stumbled backwards, leaning against the wall, looking desperately around her. Lampieur came closer to her, and she breathed hard as though she felt suffocated.

He caught her by the arms and shook her.

"I shall scream out," she said, laboring for breath. "I shall scream . . . don't touch me, don't touch me. . . ."

"I should if I wanted to," he said. "I don't want to, do you hear me? I don't care what you do. I'll frighten you to death if I like. It wouldn't matter if I did. Only don't you start screaming." He came towards her with his hands held out at her throat.

"Don't you start screaming to amuse yourself. I warn you not to give one whimper. . . ."

He seemed to be going to trample her to the ground, and Léontine sank forward, unconscious.

# CHAPTER 8

When Léontine returned to consciousness, the long empty street conveyed nothing to her mind, and she made no attempt to explain to herself why she was there. The rain fell heavily, as she sat up, holding her head between her hands, and after a little she felt about on the ground for her bag and drew her coat closer round her. She was wringing wet, and as she got on to her knees, she realized that she was unable to stand up. She sank back again, leaning against the wall, and began to remember what had happened to her and recognized the street. Her teeth chattered and she shuddered, clasping her coat round her.

"Oh God, oh God!" she said despairingly.

She imagined that Lampieur was hiding in the shadows, and yet he did not seem to be there. The darkness of the street made it impossible to make certain, but it was a relief to think him gone, and she felt calmer again.

"Are you there?" she called.

A good distance from where she was, the road forked into a further road where the streetlamps were strong and clear, and lighted up the houses outside. It was possible to see people who passed, like small silhouettes. She craned forward, watching.

"That's it," she said. "The Rue Dussoubs."

Dragging herself to her feet, she followed the street. On her right were the markets, and as she drew nearer, the noise and the shouting voices inside awoke a queer, external element in her, which was part of the nightlife she lived. The ragpickers with their strident cries were gathering in from the outskirts of Paris and obscure little bistros began to open; stray carts leased out for the night as fugitive shelters gave up their occupants like graves on the day of judgment. Fruit sellers collected to buy the stuff for their barrows, and dense masses of people thronged inside the huge building.[4] She mixed with the crowd, and came back to herself again, looking at the people and the stacks of vegetables and fruit. She even forgot Lampieur, but an overwhelming sense of utter fatigue came slowly upon her, and she stumbled along like an animal under an over-heavy load.

"Look out," a man carrying a sack on his back shouted to her. "Look out there."

"Mind yourself," a man on his heels called as he passed.

"She's down," a third, who was helping to unload a cart, said indifferently.

She heard them all laugh, without taking any real heed of them. She had been working her way through the mass of jostling people to get towards the opening nearest to the cabaret where Fouasse would be still open, and the huge man with the heaviest sack of the three looked back over his shoulder. "She's in the mud," he repeated.

---

[4] Les Halles, the vast central marketplace of Paris, which served as the principal hub for the sale and distribution of food from the Middle Ages until its redevelopment in the late twentieth century. In 1922 it was still a bustling complex of pavilions and outdoor markets, active day and night. Carco would no doubt have been familiar with Emile Zola's novel *Le Ventre de Paris* (The Belly of Paris; 1873), which offers a panoramic depiction of Les Halles and renders it as one of the book's central "characters."

She picked herself up. "I'm all right," she said. "I'm not hurt."

They only laughed again.

Keeping on, she went down the Rue Grande-Truanderie[5] as she had intended to, and on by the narrow street, Pierre-Lescot, passing open bars, market folk, slinking, ragged beggars, and unhappy-looking people who seemed ashamed to be seen and hid themselves in doorways. An evil-smelling sea of raw humanity. Motor lorries tore along, carrying butcher's meat, regardless of foot passengers, or filled with animals on the way to the slaughterhouses. She began to run suddenly, to cover the short distance between her and the cabaret.

Usually at that hour, which was well after midnight, the place was nearly empty, but because of the police drive, no one had ventured out.

"It's Léontine," some of the women greeted her, and she came to a table where Renée and Madame Berthe

---

[5] "The Rue de la Grande-Truanderie dates back to at least the thirteenth century, appearing in records as early as 1250. At that time, it was an important thoroughfare in what was then called the Quartier des Halles, near the bustling central marketplace of Paris…. The street runs along the side of the Saint-Leu-Saint-Gilles church. There are at least two interpretations of the origins of its name:

Some historians such as Sauval and Cenalis suggest it derives from 'truant,' an old term meaning 'beggar' or 'rogue,' indicating the area's association with vagrants and fortune tellers. Others like Jaillot believe it comes from 'truage,' meaning 'taxes,' as there was reportedly a bureau on the street where import duties were collected on goods entering Paris." Parishistoryproject.blogspot.com.

sat with Thérèse and Lilas. They offered her a drink and began to talk in subdued voices.

"Where have you been?" Madame Berthe asked.

"Did they give you a wash in the police station?" Lilas said with a stifled giggle of laughter.

"Not likely. I cleared out," Léontine explained.

"You know that they caught Gilberte?"

"And Yvette, with her." Renée stuck her cigarette in the corner of her mouth.

"And Margaret with her wooden leg," Madame Berthe said, nodding impressively.

"They packed her along with the rest."

"Filthy brutes," Lilas said in her thick Breton voice.

"I've been saying," Renée added, putting her shawl round her, "that this quarter is getting a bit too much of it. They never leave us alone. There's no peace."

"No, there's no peace at all," Léontine agreed. She was sitting close to the stove, her coat open.

"Ever since they murdered that old woman in the Rue Saint-Denis it's been the same thing," Lilas went on. "And I suppose it will go on like this. It's we who get the knocks."

"So we do," Madame Berthe said truculently.

"As if whoever it was, had gone shares with us,' Fat Thérèse said with a laugh. "What hopes!"

Léontine said nothing. She looked down at her draggled skirt and drenched, broken shoes hidden under her chair. If she took any notice of their complaints she might say too much. The shadow of Lampieur fell on her, frightening her again and making her thoughts incoherent. She couldn't talk of her own feelings about it. It was true that Lampieur had killed the old woman, and he depended on her for his safety. Yet the recollection of the way he had treated her gave her a dim kind of resentment against him. The fact that he had murdered someone hardly affected her at all. She knew it. It was a fact, a thing which had happened. There was no question of any principle involved. Principles were unknown to the girl, and seemed to belong to the activities of people such as the police. She had no wish to range herself on that side of the line, having suffered too much at their hands herself.

"I'd rather die," she said to herself.

As she thought of it, giving the idea a kind of shape in her mind, she saw that in any case it would be too late to speak. They would ask her why she had not come before and given information and say she was an accomplice.

"Of course he may have cleared out of here," Renée said.

Léontine shook and shivered, looking at her blankly.

"What do you think about it?" Lilas asked.

"I think so too," she said hurriedly.

## CHAPTER 9

Out of all her experiences of the night one thing remained with Léontine. She suffered, and a kind of defiance possessed her, because now she definitely feared the police. She believed that they watched her, and she suspected traps and snares on every side. When she was at the cabaret she fancied that strangers there took a special interest in her; if they came several nights in succession, or if they did not return, she was equally agitated and affected by them. Then, Lampieur left off coming, and never put his foot inside the door. She hung about near the bistro where he usually ate his evening meal, but he did not go there any longer. He had changed his restaurant. That was the simple explanation, but for her it all looked sinister and alarming. She could not go out without being attacked by waves of fear at some quite insignificant incident, and she wondered whether it might not be better to leave the quarter.

She had a furnished apartment near the Gare de l'Est, and the big boulevards offered her plenty of choice. But there, as in the other quarters, the police made their rounds, and knew every woman who lived in those streets. What could she tell them? She was alone, with no one to take her part. It would be taking a risk, and the idea of a risk unnerved her. She felt that her luck had gone. Full of all the superstition of her kind, she could not summon up enough courage to take a definite step. Partly from fatalism, and partly from sheer lassitude, she did nothing at all, and stayed on where she was.

"Hullo," Lampieur said, "so it's you?"

He was in the basement and spoke to her through the air hole where she was bending forward. She had thrown down the string and called to him.

"What do you want? Bread?"

"Three-pence worth." She saw him stoop.

"Throw down the money," he called up at her.

She obeyed him, but did not move away.

"What do you want now?" he asked roughly.

He caught the string which hung against the wall, and as he spoke it fell at his feet.

"I didn't mean to do it," she screamed down, and he could tell from her voice that she was wildly panic-stricken. "It slipped out of my hand when you pulled it." Lampieur said nothing in reply. "You didn't think I meant to do it?" she asked again. "Shall I come down and fetch it?"

"Come down," he agreed.

When she drew back from the air hole, and got up, her first thought was one of flight. It was no use thinking of that. She opened the door of the bakery, that creaked and groaned as she pushed it, and shutting it behind her, went towards the staircase.

The shop was in its usual semidarkness. Long rays of light came from the basement as though thrown by a projector, while the rest of the room remained in a kind of lamplit twilight.

"Come down," Lampieur called. A shadow eclipsed the light suddenly and swung up the walls of the shop.

"I know, I'm coming," she said timidly, holding the rope which served as a banister. "I don't want to put you out," she said.

"You won't put me out." She was touched by a kindness in his manner, and he bent and picked up the bread from the earthen floor.

"There," he said, handing it to her, "that's yours. Take it."

She looked round. "Isn't anything different here?" she asked.

"Nothing." He looked at her closely. "It's you who are changed."

"I?"

"Yes, you."

"That's rubbish," she stammered awkwardly. "Don't talk to me like that. How am I changed?"

He leaned against the wall of the cellar and watched her with slow, heavy scrutiny. "You have come back," he said, "and because you're here, you can't be afraid of me."

"I am." She cringed a little.

He gave a chuckling laugh. "I shouldn't have thought it," he said, and then with a change of manner he spoke again. "It's not too hot here, is it? Take off your coat. Don't you want to? I tell you, take off your coat." He came a little closer to her. "You have plenty of time. Now that you are here we may as well talk."

She took off her old coat and handed it to him, and he hung it on the back of a door. "That's the log shed," he explained. "I go to sleep there sometimes when I'm very tired."

Léontine looked round the thick walls that closed her in like a prison. It was stiflingly hot, and no sound would ever penetrate to the world outside in the street above them. "Even if I screamed, no one would hear me," she thought with a shiver. "Even if I screamed . . ."

"What are you doing behind the door?" she asked, summoning up sufficient courage to put the question.

"Gathering up logs."

He reappeared after a short silence, doubled up with the load he carried in his arms, and threw the wood on to the ground noisily.

"It eats money," he said, looking at the stove, "night and day, you'd ever think what it costs me. Look at that,"—he pointed to the woodshed. "A pile like that burns through in three or four days."

She could see the rows of cut logs, one piled on the other in level stacks, and a smell of pine woods and moss filtered out, cool and fresh.

"And what's that?" she asked, pointing to something which was covered up in a corner.

"My bed," he said.

She turned away quickly. There was something in his voice when he spoke that acted upon her as though he had struck her suddenly. She could not mistake his meaning.

"Let's come out," she said restlessly.

It was like going back into a fire to return to the cellar and she experienced a sense of suffocation.

"I ought to be going," she repeated, to drive back the feeling of giddiness that made her eyes swim. He was looking at her with steady fixity and did not stir.

"Give me my coat."

"Your coat?"

"Give it to me."

"Wait," he said slowly. He seemed to be fighting with himself, and the inward battle showed in his eyes. "You wanted your coat, didn't you?"

"I must go." She spoke with entreaty.

"You can't," he said. "Not until after . . ."

"After what?" Her face was scared.

"It's a suggestion I'd like to make," he said, speaking as though he was trying to put his thoughts into intelligible order. "A kind of arrangement between us. That's if you like. . . ." He made an exasperated gesture. "Think it over and tell me. Were you glad to see me again?"

"You might have some pity." Her voice quavered and broke up suddenly.

"There's not much pity anywhere," he said harshly. "Do you hear me? Since the other night I've been thinking how frightened you were, and I don't like frightening you. I'm not as bad as all that. No, I'm not really as bad as that. So I thought about it. . . . You see, I'm always alone, even at the bistro, and I said to myself, here it is, it's like this, I said I wouldn't have you afraid of me. You believe that, don't you?"

She drew back from him.

"You don't believe me?" he said with a kind of puzzled surprise at her. "I'm sorry I frightened you badly. I couldn't get it out of my head all the night. Do you hear? I couldn't. And next day I thought it over again, and I saw that you had come here after me, and there was something already. . . ."

"What?" she asked in a weak voice. "What was there?"

"Things," he said, speaking louder. "The next day I didn't dare to go looking about for you, I was ashamed to do a thing like that. You can see that much, can't you? I couldn't go hunting for you to come and speak to me, and for those days and nights I was here alone like a madman. It was your fault I got like that. Do you understand me? The trouble came back to me, and I couldn't go up into the street. I worked, and stuck it out, because I'd said you were to come here."

"I never wanted to come," she said doubtfully.

"But you came, for all that. I knew you would. I could have sworn it. I was glad."

He lifted his head strangely. "Don't answer me straight away. Think it over. Take your time. Take until tomorrow night. You have only to pass the bakery."

"And if I tell you at once?" she asked in a voice of disgust.

Lampieur swung his body backwards and forwards. "If you do you must say what I want," he said dully, pulling his belt tighter round his loose trousers, and looking quietly at her.

She watched him, with an ashy-white face, pinched and thin. Her voice died away when she tried to speak, and something in her throat swelled, and half choked her.

"Well?" he asked. "Is it yes?" He came a step towards her and she watched him coming without moving from where she stood.

"It is yes?" he repeated.

She realized suddenly that he was stripped to the waist, and saw his arms, his body, the light falling on his naked shoulders. A feeling of shame, which she had never experienced before, and a loathing of him overwhelmed her. It was too late. He caught her and pressed her close to him.

"What more do you want of me?" she asked.

## CHAPTER 10

When she awoke in the morning in Lampieur's room, Léontine looked around her. All the prostitute's horror was upon her, the horror of all men, impersonated in the body of one. A beaten sense of utter humiliation added to her shame and self-disgust, and yet she had not fallen so low as to have submitted voluntarily to the will of Lampieur.

She had no choice. A series of wretched accidents or events had resulted in this, and now she must try to make the best of it, since it was her fault that it had been possible. Having got as far as that, Léontine thought afresh of the awful fatality which had caught her, and tried to prepare herself for fresh trouble. She had given herself to Lampieur out of fear, and because she thought he was going to terrify her again, and even put his threats into execution. What could she have done against him?

She recalled the cellar with the white-washed walls, the silence down there, and the isolation. Why had she ever gone down the staircase? She couldn't remember what had brought her. Everything that had happened yesterday was vague and indistinct, but she recalled her own craving to go and look down the air hole, to lean over, and shout to Lampieur. It had possessed her, gained hold of her mind, driven her body onwards, and swamped her will. That had been the real cause of all that happened.

In the very room where she was, out of the result of her own act, she had a strange feeling that she had in some way lost herself for a time, and returned again to discover that she and this other self of hers were one and the same. A confused sense of astonishment pierced her.

"To think of that," she said to herself.

Beside her, dead weary, Lampieur lay in a dense sleep, breathing with heavy snoring gasps. If only she could escape, as he did, from the torment she endured. She could not. Whenever she tried to lie with her eyes shut, she fell back into the same trouble. "It's like that . . ." she repeated over and over again. "I can't do anything. It's like that."

The room was small and ill-kept. Cigarette ends lay on the dirty planks. A trunk did duty as a table, and the light came in through a skylight, hard, raw and blinding. She turned from it all to look again at Lampieur, watched him for a long time and then closed her eyes, forcing herself not to think of him. He drew a heavy breath and moved. Instinctively Léontine moved away, afraid that she had awakened him, and pretended to sleep.

"What?" he asked, speaking thickly in his sleep. "What . . . You have been waiting for me?" He choked and fought for breath. "I . . . know—nothing. . . ." His voice became incoherent, only registering the terror that lay over his mind.

"There, there," she said to quiet him, and shook him gently to recall him from the world of his dream. "It is me," she said. "Don't you see me?"

"Yes." He sat up in the bed and looked at her.

"You've been awake?" he asked her in a strange voice.

"I didn't sleep," she admitted.

He gave her a guarded look, and appeared to forget her again.

She sat up beside him, and could not take her eyes from his face. He did not yet seem to realize that she was there, but she could tell from movements of his forehead and eyebrows that he was weighing something connected with her in his mind, and the look he eventually shot at her was one of challenge and suspicion.

"Aren't we ever going to get up and go out?" she asked.

In reply he lurched out of the bed, thrust his feet into his old slippers and pulling on a pair of trousers, went to the table and began to wash. She followed him with her stricken, fascinated look. He plunged his head into cold water and dried himself, carrying through every detail of his toilet with a peculiarly minute attention, the concentration of a man who is not perfectly sure of himself. As he emptied the dirty water into a bucket he spoke to her.

"Yes, we can go out," he agreed, and gave up his place at the basin to Léontine, who got up and began to dress.

It was about three o'clock in the afternoon, and the light in the room was clear and level, but already beginning to change a little. Lampieur looked at his watch, then he put it back into his pocket, and opened the window. His expression of settled worry gave place to something stronger, a more resolute sadness.

But he kept his own secret. He walked about the room, got up and sat down, went backwards and forwards, always avoiding Léontine silently. He hated her. He measured the space between them carefully and thought of the thousand terrors she had made him suffer. He saw her outside, slinking along the walls. He saw her in the cellar, and all these impressions of her concentrated into one, which he could not drive off. Against this one conception of her, the presence of the girl herself, actually there in the room with him, was quite unreal. He watched her, he wanted to hunt her away if he could.

Léontine was dressing, standing by the bed, and he reproached himself for all he had done the night before. He had not the smallest further desire for her, his senses were dead and dull. Had he ever really desired her? He did not understand. What morbid, unwholesome craving had driven him towards her, what perverted longing? He cast it aside, sickened. His one thought was to get her out of his room, go with her into the street and, once there, find some excuse for leaving her, never to see her again.

Yet, directly they were in the street together, they were conscious of an insurmountable difficulty for either of them to leave the other. The same shame and the same fear hemmed them in, and neither had the courage to risk the consequence of settling the question.

People were hurrying along all round them, motorbuses boomed past with their deafening noise, the very clamor of the street made it impossible to speak without shouting. And then it was still clear daylight, the sun's rays fell on the facades of houses and under colonnades, it hung there in the sky like a dull halo. If it hadn't been for that, the daylight and the sun, the noise and the crashing of wheels, Lampieur might have spoken.

"Later on will be best," he said, putting his hand over his face.

"Are we going to Fouasse?" Léontine asked.

"No," he said. "This way." He pointed to the opposite direction from the cabaret.

"I ought to go back to my lodging," she said.

"All right. Go. Is it far?"

"Some way."

"I'll come along," he said, and he walked with her, turning to the left along the Boulevard Sebastopol, where the shop windows were beginning to light up.

At that hour the streets were crowded.

The tramcars slid along their rails, in arrows of light. Police at the widest crossings held up the traffic for the foot passengers to cross, and then again the process repeated itself.

Night fell. Here and there along benches under the trees, women whose beauty was gone, and who were battered and repugnant to look at, sat waiting for customers. Others hung about around the shops, and sandwich men made their weary procession onwards. Pale street boys walked about with young prostitutes, who dodged in and out among the passersby. They laughed with their wide, painted mouths, and their eyes were full of sly invitation.

"Is it much further?" Lampieur asked.

Léontine did not hear him. She was getting well into the crowd and had forgotten him. He might follow her if he liked. Lampieur, for her, was not the man who walked beside her. She thought of the other

Lampieur who had murdered an old woman, and who made her sick with horror of him. How was she to escape him? She had tried that already, and had gone back. She might do it again, call him again and go down the cellar with him. The night before, it had happened so. She did not forget anything and as though to pass all former boundaries, Lampieur had captured, and at once drawn back from her. He had looked at her with contempt.

## CHAPTER 11

What Léontine could not put out of her mind was, that the situation which existed between her and Lampieur had not arisen out of anything which could remotely be described as love. It was gross desire, nothing could lessen that fact. She could drape it about with no illusion. If Lampieur had told her in so many words what it was which drove him, she could have understood it, since her own restless torment sprang from the same cause. She saw how the affair stood, and could blame no one. It was like that. . . . Their common fate decreed it, and you couldn't escape, just as you couldn't escape from the ordinary necessary events of the day.

Plunged in her own bitter reflections, she went up the street, Lampieur behind her. They did not speak, but kept along, side by side, looking at nothing, but drifting with the crowd.

"My God!" Lampieur said. He stopped for a second, and as Léontine went onwards without noticing, he caught her up again, wondering why he had not taken his chance
escape.

"What's the matter?" he asked.

He was wounded in his self-conceit, and offended because Léontine did not look round at once. "You'll see," he said inwardly. "You'll see. This won't go on for long."

He began to think out obscure and hostile plans towards her, and he trudged behind her angrily. She represented the first move towards an end which, since he awoke in the room, he had known that he was steadily approaching. What the end was, he could not yet tell. Neither did he realize that the thoughts he nursed blackly against her dated back long before that moment. He believed that his loathing for Léontine, and the secret longing he felt to hurt and damage her, to make her suffer and go on suffering, only began when he became aware that this was how he felt. He was strangely blind to the truth that ever since the murder he had hated her, and that out of this there had arisen his desire to humiliate her. Hatred had given birth to lust . . . only he could not understand.

She called out to him as he followed the dark windings of his thoughts, and he stopped with a jerk.

"Are we there?" he asked.

"Yes, this is the place."

He looked up at the dirty entrance, the narrow staircase and a lamp with a white globe on which the word "Hotel" was printed in black letters. They looked at one another and he made up his mind.

"Go on," he said. "I'll come with you."

He took her by the arm and they walked up past the first floor. Her room was on the fourth landing and the windows looked out over a courtyard and the kitchen premises of a furnished block of flats. It was dark and shut in, and even at midday would have been shadowed by the upper stories of the building. The window fastened badly, and a ragged curtain sagged over it, and the boards of the floor were irregular and worm-eaten. Léontine lighted the oil lamp and tugged the curtain across, while Lampieur slammed the door, and she threw her coat on the bed.

"It's big," he said.

"What?"

"The room." He sat down on a chair and took off his hat, saying no more. He was staring at the red flame of the lampwick, because something he had not thought of before occurred to him suddenly, and surprised him. He began to realize that as well as being the woman who had guessed his secret, Léontine had a life of her own, outside of that. He saw the room, the bed, the lamp, the wretched curtain that hardly hid the window, and tried to gather in this new idea of her. Even if she had a life of her own, how could it affect anything? Every human being, however isolated, however dependent, has an individual life, — he had, himself . . . only he had been living away from reality for so long in a world of suspicion and fear that he could no longer keep count of the woes and terrors which haunted him.

Why doesn't he say anything? Léontine tried to imagine the reason. As he was there, why couldn't he speak? His silence began to break her nerve, it was alarming to her. What could she have been thinking of to let him come there? He was behaving so strangely that she wondered if he were mad.

He got up and lowered the lampwick which had flared in the draught, and then looked curiously at everything on the mantelpiece, taking up a photograph of a small child.

"That's yours?" he asked. "Your own?"

"Dead," Léontine said.

He put down the photograph and began to walk about the room.

"Died three years ago," Léontine went on. "He was with people I'd paid to take care of him in the country."

"When was it?"

"After I'd left home. It was because of him I cleared off. They didn't want me there. Father turned me out."

"And your mother?" he asked.

"Never had one that I remember. And you?"

"Oh, they're still there," he said in a grumbling voice. "The old people go on the same in the same way. They're still there," he repeated, his eyes looking at some inward picture the words recalled to him. And then she saw a sudden gleam pierce through the shadow of his memory and blaze out for a second, filling her with instinctive fear of him, as he burst into a dreadful laugh.

"What?" he asked. "Have I been jabbering?"

"I don't know what you mean," she said reluctantly, fearing to draw his anger towards her. "Don't you remember at all what you said?"

"I spoke of the old people," he said harshly. "When I do that it makes me think of myself. They were hard. . . . It's past and over now, all that time, and a good thing it is."

"Then don't think of it," she suggested.

"That's it." He spoke half to himself. "Yes, that's it; still, there are things one remembers."

"That's funny," she said blankly.

"Dirty things. . . ."

"That's the same for us all," she agreed.

# CHAPTER 12

All the memories he had which were oven round Léontine kept him prisoner in the grubby room in the hotel. His whole world seemed enclosed by it, and it exasperated his mind. He foresaw a danger to himself if he began to talk confidences with her. She would sit there and draw him out. He gave her a slow look of hatred. It was a good thing he had thought of that in time.

"What are you going to do now?" he asked.

"Nothing," she replied listlessly.

"There's nothing you can do. . . . It's failed, that scheme you had."

"What?" She stared wide-eyed at him.

"I saw through it. Did you think I'd not?"

She shook her head in bewilderment.

"Come now." He faced her. "First of all, why do you come here? It wasn't to make me follow you?"

"No."

"And that photo on the mantelpiece. . . . Look at it, of course that wasn't put there for me, of course not? It's an old trick, that dead baby dodge. They sell them in the shops round here. . . ."

"Hold your tongue," she cried shrilly at him. "What right have you to say such things to me? You followed me. It wasn't my fault."

"That's very likely, isn't it?" he jeered at her.

"Then prove it. Prove it."

"Oh, go to hell with your proof."

"The proof is,"—she stuck to her point,—"that I wanted to get rid of you, to get away from you."

"What?"

"Get away from you," she said with sudden energy. "Anywhere, just away from you, somewhere where I could forget. . . ."

He jumped up from his chair. "You say that?" He came over towards her. "Listen. You're a liar. No one forgets. I say that you are a liar, you tell lies, and that one goes on remembering. You want to leave me so that I shall be alone, so that I shall go crazy again, and then go looking for you. . .

"Don't persecute me," she said, drawing away.

"Last night it was you who came back," he went on. "You threw down the string. You shouted to me to come. Didn't you? You let go the string on purpose. You can't deny that, as it's true." He came towering over her, trampling the floor with his heavy tread. "What have you to say? Answer me. I want to know what you mean, why you came, what you want. . . ."

"Don't come nearer." She warded him off with her fragile little hands, and he stopped dead.

He had driven her backwards against the foot of the bed, and she stood there watching him so fixedly that he could not bear the steadiness of her look.

"Clear out," she said. "Get away from here. Leave me alone. You want to do something dreadful to me."

She bowed forward and hid her face in her hands, and he stood there clumsily, speechless and abashed. It was he who had wanted to rid himself of her, and never to set eyes on her again, and now he realized that on her side she hated him. It wounded him in a way that he could not express. She humbled him in his own eyes, his very sex suffered the ignominy of her loathing for him. It was insupportable.

As she hung there limply, waiting for him to go, he saw that he still had the power in his own hands. She hadn't an ounce of fight left.

"All right," he said sulkily. "If that is how you want it." He put on his hat and went towards the door. "We've agreed on that. To live as I'd arranged in my mind that we might, doesn't do."

She lifted her head and sighed heavily.

"Don't begin that," he spoke sharply.

"It's happened to others before now. We tried, and it didn't do."

"Why do you say that?" she asked.

"Because . . ." He looked around the room at the walls and the rickety furniture with a strange, long look. "Every one has to live as best suits them. That's it, isn't it?"

He was perfectly sincere as he spoke; he knew that he held on to Léontine, not only on account of the fact that she had it in her power to denounce him, but because it gave him a sense of pleasure to revenge himself on her for his sufferings. No other feeling merged into this. He was pitiless, and in that lay his power.

Still he did not go, and she did not force him to open the door and leave her. New chains had been forged around them, drawing them together again by their strong, invisible force.

## CHAPTER 13

A strange life began for them from the time when they had been unable to separate one from the other. Léontine lived at the bakery. That is to say, she waited for Lampieur until morning at a bar near the market until he fetched her, and then they went back to his room to sleep. In the evenings they dined together in the Rue Saint-Denis, and Lampieur went to his work, while Léontine straggled about in the streets, as she always had, up to midnight, when they met at the cabaret, and he stood her a drink.

No one said anything. It all seemed quite natural. They all knew that Lampieur was a good, steady workman, who earned his living hard. He had the right to amuse himself if he liked. But Léontine's comrades of former times thought it a little unusual when they discussed it together, and they scented mystery.

They felt that there was something queer behind it. The haggard eyes and look of Lampieur, his suggestion of inward trouble, and Léontine's reserve when they were together struck them all.

They were both so extraordinarily punctual at their meeting places, and there was no look of gladness or gaiety when they did meet. They sat together without speaking a word. A kind of mutual indifference isolated them completely. Even when Lampieur called the waiter and paid for what they had eaten and drunk, it was noticed that he left Léontine without so much as saying good-night to her, while she sat as if she was lost in an uncanny dream.

It was a bad dream, they felt. But they only saw a fragment of the life, and that, from outside. They might have said more if they could have followed them to the bakery and up to the room where they slept.

Lampieur was the first to get into bed, and he watched Léontine as he lay there, and did not speak to her, and then he turned over and slept. She followed him noiselessly and lay beside him in a deathly stillness until her eyes closed and she slid away into the nightmare mockery of rest and sleep. Even in their dreams they were dragged through strange places trying to find something irrevocably lost, and so great was the strain on Léontine's nerves, of the abominable necessity which forced them to shelter together, that on awaking, sometimes she clung to Lampieur crying hopelessly and helplessly in his arms.

For him, his eyes staring open, he could see vague forms of the things which had haunted and hunted him in his dreams. The world which he knew to be real was dissolving, and Léontine was quite powerless to help him or rescue him any longer.

In the streets, in the bars where they sat, nothing could get through to them from outside. Even the people who they knew were watching them were incoherent and meant nothing whatever. Lampieur took no heed of them and behaved with a mechanical rudeness to them all. In some way he got through his work, like an automaton who performs a set task each night at a regular hour. His body went to and fro in the cellar, but his spirit was no longer there.

There were times when he forgot Léontine, and she also became as nothing at all to him. But the most serious fact which menaced him was that he began to try to recall the murder. Already, five or six times he had been obliged to pull himself together and make a huge effort of memory to admit that he, Lampieur the baker, had actually committed a murder. It was as though he were the sport of an obsession, not to understand that he had. Yet each detail came to his rescue, and he grew aware that his consciousness registered it all with awful lucidity.

He began, out of this, to reconstruct all that had happened, and to picture the facts afresh. It worried him constantly, as he tried to recall what had decided him to take the step. He could not be certain. Was it the old woman's money? Was it a longing for some kind of risk, or adventure? Both together possibly, but there was another element as well as something that was deep down in his nature, an obscure sadic instinct that now awoke once more in the case of Léontine.

As for her, she didn't know anything of this. She thought he was brutalized and hard because he had murdered the old woman, and that made her sorry for him. She had even tried to imagine the murder so as to share his suffering a little better. A doglike devotion began to awake in her. She lived with him, he would keep her there always. It meant pathetically much in her life, and had a hundred consolations for her. She accepted any treatment from him without complaint. When they went to Fouasse and he left her without a word, she knew the others noticed it. She was not angry. She watched him go, with a resigned sweetness in her blue eyes, humbly ready to take upon herself any sacrifice if she could shelter him. She wanted him to rest, and would willingly have relinquished any comfort from her own life to be of use to him.

The only tranquility she was able to experience herself was miserable and scanty enough, if any such term could be applied to the anxiety she suffered. She got up and followed him out of the bar. Far from harboring any feeling of reproach against him for having made her a slave, she was willing and even grateful. Through him she had an object in her forlorn existence, and it had redeemed her. In some strange way the new experience purified and dimly ennobled her, conquering her sad knowledge, and wiping out the stains of her daily life. Out of her forgotten girlhood, an old dream revived, an ideal she had once caught a glimpse of, as of a burning light, far above her. It was very simple, but she raised her face towards it once again, and in its shining she was able to put aside regret; she even had a fierce satisfaction in realizing the need there was for her day by day to prepare to pay the price for her own transfiguration. This presentment of herself was no longer at war with the other Léontine, who fashioned her life. She raised herself insensibly to a different level. A deep, hidden joy mixed in with the trouble, attaching itself to Lampieur, and filling her with gratitude towards him out of his fulfillment of her need for love.

In the streets at night Léontine's strangely achieved sense of happiness bore her up. She saw Lampieur in her mind working in the cellar and she watched him.

The thought of the murder haunted her, but not with horror, as she was so well used to it. It was done, and there was no changing that. More than this, it was the one way she could identify herself with Lampieur and be with him if a moment came to face the consequences of his crime. The consequences were ghastly to think of, but they had also the inexplicable attraction of chastisement and an all-conquering truth which cannot be escaped.

She knew this. She knew too that rough and blunted as he was, Lampieur might come to realize as she had herself the compelling power exercised upon all sinners, by atonement. It was dreadful to think of this. She could not submit to it, and fought wildly against the thought which forced itself upon her, feeling that in doing so she diverted any secret movement of his mind towards the same deadly attraction that called to her.

Even though she was determined to protect him from this danger, she had never dared to warn him of it. What was the use? When he was there she was self-conscious and lost all assurance. She was never easy with him. Amid all the intimacy of their life, they had never been able to speak openly, or even to talk of foolish little things together. Under ordinary, simple words, strange allusions might slide in. . . . Ambiguous questionings. . . . Lampieur would never allow it. Having made his own unlucky confidence to Léontine, he held his tongue, or if he did speak to her, it was reluctantly, and she felt utterly discouraged by him. There was no way by which she could persuade him to listen to her. Léontine kept her fears to herself and spoke of them to no one.

## CHAPTER 14

She became more and more frightened at the thought that Lampieur would awaken as she had, to the fascination that swept her when she thought of the murder and its consequences. She lingered about near the bakery all night, as he worked, believing that the fact of her being there protected him. At least she told herself that she believed it, for it was the only comfort she had in her days.

In her dreams she helped him out of traps, saved him from ambush, and gave him new courage. These dreams meant so much to her. They illuminated the drabness of the hours spent face to face with him. He would put up with her better, she felt, if he knew her touching desire to be of service to him. But of all that she could never speak. . . .

She made her wandering round past the bakery, watching and stopping, coming back and going off a little further again. Three houses up the street there was a bar where she sat, and from where, without anyone noticing her, she could keep her eyes on the street and be able to warn him of danger. In the bar, as the nights dragged on, she often found herself overtaken by a fierce pity towards him which she sank down before, sitting there among the men and women who drank and took no notice of her. There was a strangeness about the very quality of this piteous sympathy, and she realized that though it punished her, it gave her a bitter, aching joy.

The men who drank in the bar were mostly river porters, and loafers who came in from the quays; old slatternly women who drank cheap red wine. They were quiet enough, and she looked at them one by one, weighed down by their separate destiny, each one hidden.

Those nights in the market! One man leaning across the counter was like a sleeping animal, harnessed to his burden and waiting for the crack of the whip to call him up to his work again. Another of them sat tracing lines on the little table before him, looking at nothing. Silence, the dead silence of utter fatigue filled the place. The atmosphere was full of it, incoherent as a bad dream, lit up by a steady and evil light.

As the nights wore through, the place attracted her more strongly. She never went anywhere else, and amid the clients, each one of them with so much individual misery, the woman who sat there relaxed and defeated was not much different to the others. She was the same as they were but for one thing. She longed to be of use to Lampieur, and to give him back hope.

It was towards the early hours of morning, Léontine felt utterly miserable. The windows of the bar began to gleam with a pale light from without. The outline of roofs beyond cleared gradually, and the sky grew pale and turned a dirty gray, a gray that spread everywhere. The gas began to flicker a little in the burners, and soon was extinguished, and far away the rumble of the first tram rent the silence and tore it into rags.

Then Lampieur opened the door of the bar, and Léontine came to life again with all the other things around, which had suddenly begun to move and grow awake and restless. They opened the shutters noisily in the shops, men passed in the street, or, like Lampieur, came in and asked for a cup of coffee, which was served on the zinc counter. She called him, and he came, sitting down beside her. A glance between them spoke of the acid satisfaction he had in seeing her there. They were together. . . . His one look comforted her. Then he signed to the bartender who had served them, and they went off without anyone having noticed them at all.

"Come on," Lampieur said.

She hurried along beside him, and walking together down the Rue des Prêcheurs, they went in at the bakery, and up to the little room under the slates, and slept.

Had she wished it, Léontine could have waited in the little room under the slates for Lampieur to come to her, instead of sitting in the bar and wearing herself out with her fears. Over and over again Lampieur had suggested it, but she felt that down there in the shop, and in the same street, she could watch over him, and know if he were threatened by any danger, whereas, in the room, she could only sit there, imagining things. . . . That would have been a thousand times worse.

Sometimes when she was actually with him in the room, she was strung up to a pitch of agony, and to be there alone would have driven her mad. The sudden longing to rush out into the streets and lose herself in Paris, attacked her; the idea of getting clear off into some other life. His being there, made her think of this, and she wondered if he had the same panic-stricken desire for flight. If he had, why did he not give way to it?

She didn't dare to think of that.

She was nothing now without Lampieur. He had dragged her out of the old life, and forced her onwards to the strange fate which, while she feared, she was physically incapable of attempting to avoid. She could not have undertaken her old métier anymore. The weight of the fatality of it all crushed her, even when he was there to share it and she could cling desperately to him. If he were to go away and try and find hope or peace apart from her, it would end everything so far as she was concerned. . . . She had lost all she had, and even when the idea beckoned to her, she was not strong enough to withdraw.

Mercifully for her, these feelings that came to her did not last, and when they came they only revealed such a lonely and hopeless future that she hugged afresh the bitter joy of things as they were. When all was said and done, Lampieur had saved her from herself. He produced in her the sense of illusion, of being young once again, and that illusion was curiously precious. Because of his crime, life had taken another shape. It was not a question of nights and days, pleasure, or even individual existence. Quite the reverse. . . . At all times alike the act he had committed kept its significance for him, as for her. It was eternally present with them both. It drifted them onwards on its slow current, and though they were always silent about it, it superimposed itself on them ceaselessly.

He had changed a great deal. His moodiness became more exaggerated and he could not always control himself. There were times when he was terrifying to her. Nights when he flung himself out of bed and put on his clothes, and a horror of distress showed in his eyes. Nothing mattered to him. He did not show any wish to live. His abasement became worse as it expressed itself, and a kind of rage stormed through him. There was no special reason for these tempests when they broke, but the smallest thing caused them, and Léontine submitted to them silently, her pity for him awakening and causing her to bow silently before the devastating anguish of his soul. He could not account for it. It came, and he was beside himself, maddened by her as she lay there with her face hidden, saying nothing, doing nothing to add to his fury.

During one of these violent attacks he poured out on her all the pent-up disgust and loathing with which she inspired him. It was her fault, he said, that his life was ruined.

Léontine listened to him. His reproaches affected her no more than the blows he struck at her to force her to speak. She knew it was not she who had ruined his life, and he knew it too. It was because he suffered so dreadfully that he acted as he did. She understood all that. . . . She never held him responsible for the wrong he did to her, and she forgave him, saying that it was not upon her, but himself that he needed revenge. Once the crisis was past, he fell back into his heavy stupor, and lost himself once more.

# CHAPTER 15

After one of these violent scenes Lampieur fell a prey to an unexpected reaction. He entreated her to forget, and at his kindness she burst into tears.

"Don't cry," he said. "Look here, Léontine, don't cry. What is it?"

"It's not my fault." She looked up with bruised eyes, red and sad.

Lampieur bent over her. "Of course not," he said, looking at her with a strange mixture of astonishment and pity. He was softened and his mind worked slowly. "Why are you crying?" he asked, as though her reply had disclosed something hidden to him.

She shook her head silently.

"There are times when I don't know what I do," he said. "Times when I break out. I'm driven to it. Things are dragged out of me. I go further than I mean."

"It's not that. I'm not crying about that," she said.

"What is it, then?"

"Other things," she said.

He left it at that and did not press her further. "Yes," he agreed dully.

An overwhelming shame came over him, because of those "other things" she had hinted at. He sat there, thinking of them.

It was evening, and the skylight showed a square of pale pink sky, calm and delicate with the shadow of the sunset still reflected on the soft clouds. He looked at it, and then he turned to her. "What other things?" he asked.

She trembled, and did not speak.

"All right," he said, hiding his feelings under a pretence of confidence. "Come on now, what do you mean by that?"

"Oh God!" She rocked herself distractedly.

"We ought to agree about those things," he argued. "Don't you see that?"

"I don't."

"I thought as much," he said irritably. "It's enough if I keep a lookout, without you being at that game too. I can't stand it. I hit out, and we go back to this, always having these rows. I tell you I can't stand it. What about you?" He put a heavy hand on her shoulder. "It's your cursed notion again, isn't it?"

He did not wait for her to answer but let his hand fall from her shoulder. "You're wrong," he said gloomily. "You oughtn't to have these notions at all. It's because of that I let out at you. Don't say it isn't. . . . Since we've been here together, there's always this notion of yours between us. What do you want me to do? I don't start defending myself, it would be no good, you'd only despise me. . . ."

She listened without interrupting him, but he had not convinced her. He said she had forced her "notion" on him, because he wanted to persuade himself that he was not responsible for his brutality. He was lying. He was taking a great deal of trouble to twist the facts and avoid the clear truth. She knew that he had committed the murder in the Rue Saint-Denis, he had as good as admitted it to her the night she fainted in the street. Every day he gave her fresh proof of it. Did he imagine that she had not realized it? It humiliated her to think that he could fool her. She considered the question. He was not trying to fool her, he had spoken like a man who is hopelessly confused in mind, and who was attempting to justify himself under accusation.

Still she said nothing. It was he who came back and back to the idea against which he fought. The defense he dwelt on was that he had been asleep the night of the crime, when Léontine threw down the coppers. He had been asleep in the woodshed where there was the settle[6] with the cover over it. That was proof enough, wasn't it? Why was it there if he didn't sleep there now and then? And he had roused himself soon enough to give sufficient proof. What had she to say that? The police might come prying round. Lampieur didn't care if they did. What were the police to him? She need only put the questions to him. He could reply, word for word. Very well, if they did suspect him, they would have taken him to the police station. At least they would have come and asked him what he had been doing that night. They'd have cross-questioned him. He'd have had a chance to speak. Instead of that, what had happened? He lived perfectly quietly, nobody troubled their heads about him. No one suspected him. Could she deny that?

"I never said it." She sat with her eyes lowered. "I never said anything."

"You," he said. "You, *you*," throwing the word at her. "Whenever you speak . . ."

"But I never speak of it."

"Hold your tongue," he shouted.

---

[6] Settle: a wooden bench with arms, a high solid back, and an enclosed foundation that can be used as a chest.

He began to walk about the room in his heavy, swinging way, abusing her in an angry voice, and looking at her savagely from time to time. She didn't take her eyes off him. Did she want another scene between them?

The pity that had swamped all her other feelings ebbed and a resentment towards him filled her. Not only did he treat her as he would not have dared to treat anyone else, but he suspected her as though she were an enemy . . . he repulsed her and warded her off. He would always treat her exactly the same, and she could not see how it would end. Even the part she played in bearing his anguish with him was unknown to him. It was all to no purpose that she spent herself, that she sheltered him without his guessing it. She was a stranger in his eyes.

He believed that she would stay with him, and he would keep her always, but only out of fear. He was afraid she might chatter and tell the others if she ever left him. He pretended to laugh and care nothing for them, and said she might go and say anything she knew, but he never forgave her for knowing it. With things as they were, she asked herself again what could be the end of it all for her? There was nothing anywhere. All she had striven towards, worked for, was useless. A huge darkness opened ahead of her, a black abyss of limitless despair. She looked down at it, and her brain swam.

"Well," he asked, "you're looking at something, I suppose?"

He thrust on his hat with a kind of horrible jauntiness that hit Léontine like a blow.

"Where are you going?" she asked.

He opened the door. "Out," he said. "You'll see where I'm going."

He went off quickly without asking her to come with him and eat their supper in the Rue Saint-Denis, which he had always done before.

# CHAPTER 16

Alone in the room, Léontine sat there very still. She had ceased to think of him as she had been thinking of him for so long.

The light was fading out and everything grew dim as the sky darkened slowly. What was she to do, now that Lampieur had gone?

Down the lighted streets, in the shabby little restaurant where he was probably sitting at a table, he might be regretting that he had left her. It was a change in all his settled way of life. . . . Would he go straight back to work? she wondered, and thought he would not. . . . She was quite free to take a decision that his going had forced upon her. It was the moment for her to make up her mind definitely.

There was nothing to expect from such a man. His grossness of nature, his hardness, broke down her resistance. She was no longer sorry for him. A sense of revenge caught her, and the feeling of release from him came with warmth and comfort to her heart. It was deliverance. After all her weariness and torment of soul, she was detached from him, and at rest. . . .

Night came on. Soft, melting and comforting it fell around Léontine and soothed her. It was one of the first nights of early spring, and it gathered her into its gentle caress.

Lampieur was leaving the restaurant by this time. What thoughts hunted him? she wondered. She pictured the street, the shop fronts and the crisscross of the lamplight. He might be walking up the street below at that very moment, not realizing that spring had come. With him nothing mattered except his own safety and his own isolation. He jeered at everything else. Even if he did feel the mystery of the night, he would arm himself against it, suspecting a secret foe.

Lampieur had come back to the bakery. Wherever he looked that night he was aware of an inexplicable lure in everything. The lights from the bistros shone on him with double strength. Along the walls the posters seemed gay and attractive. He noticed them and read the advertisements; the very pavement felt different and he walked lightly.

He amused himself with this new sensation. It gave him a queer pleasure to feel interested, and he saw that having broken with Léontine was the real cause of the change. Directly he thought of her, his happy mood vanished and he became angry, and he thought of her bitterly as he walked slowly again, mounting the street. The lights and the flaming posters had ceased to give him any pleasure.

As this inward chill and change touched his lighter mood, Léontine, alone in the room up the staircase, had decided. She was going to leave Lampieur and live as best she might until her energy revived.

And yet the thought of his return to the empty room, the loneliness that waited for him, touched and saddened her. She found it unbearable. Try as she would, she could not get used to it, so that it did not hurt her. Try as she would when she had dressed herself, she could not go out of the door. . . . Her determination failed her.

The door opened at last, and all she had to do was to shut it behind her and she could run away.

But could she ?

Never before had she felt him so close to her as when she mixed with the crowd in the street. Her will to leave him had been strung up to a point where it deserted her suddenly like a faithless friend. It no longer sustained her and she knew that she was powerless to escape from the future.

## CHAPTER 17

Of all the evenings of her life, this one was marked for Léontine as being the most tormented and distressing. She went to the cabaret kept by Fouasse, and waited for Lampieur, sitting among the other women. He did not come. At midnight she dragged along the Rue Saint-Denis and began to follow her usual road. Light streamed upwards through the air hole telling her he was there, and she came back once or twice, passing by without stopping before she caught sight of him below her in the cellar.

One o'clock struck and she was still there. She went on again up the road and down on the further side, the street yawning emptily to the sky. Now and then figures passed her hurrying towards the market, caught into the light at a corner and lost again. Others came out from the opposite direction and flickered silhouette-like for an instant and were gone. Prostitutes, hidden in the doorways, moved out and stopped and spoke to men who came towards them. She saw them all with extraordinary clearness, and, at the farthest end of the street, there were two policemen who walked together slowly past the cabaret and a taxicab that stopped in front of the lighted entrance to a hotel.

The taxi, the policemen and the four or five prostitutes, and now and then a passerby, made no real difference to the sleeping street. They rather intensified something drowsy and stagnant in the atmosphere. The idea struck her, and she began to walk cautiously, imitating the people she followed with her eyes, and it gave her a sensation of something unusual and disconnected. All around her the shop fronts and the houses stood up towering to the dark sky, and in the narrow alleys everything slept. She went on, held in the same flat calm.

She did not try to test this deep feeling of well-being, it gave her a sensuous joy, and hope dawned dimly in her mind. After all, she reasoned, no danger threatened Lampieur and she began to believe that in the morning he would come to the bar, just as usual, to fetch her and bring her home with him.

When she came to the entrance of the bar, she paused. At the far side of the road she could see the entrance of the house where the murder had been committed, with its mean, dingy door. The very sight of it caused her to move away quickly, filled with a sudden disgust which always attacked her when she passed that way. It frightened her.

It was just the same as all the other houses, shabby and dirty. The entrance with its brown door, which had never been left open since the night of the murder, attracted no special attention. By day it was possible to see the long corridor, the narrow walls and the worn steps of the staircase, the glass panes of the concierge's lodge. Léontine remembered these details, there was nothing distinctive in it anywhere. Only now that the door was closed, there was something funereal and mournful about the house. The shut *volets*,[7] the heavy outline lent it a strange effect.

She wondered that no one noticed it. . . . Lampieur had avoided having to pass it for a whole month, and she wondered if he too would find it horrible to look

---

[7] Volets: shutters.

at. Several times as they had crossed the road to avoid it, she had known that he shivered with a kind of instinctive dread.

No one else, except themselves, would know that the house appeared to be waiting for something. No one else would guess that, or think why she was frightened, because it only affected her and Lampieur, and took a definite shape to them, brooding with its unutterable power. It was not the first time Léontine had told herself this, but it disconcerted her and seemed to leap upon her afresh, loosing a host of vague presentiments. She gave way to them, standing before the house where the old woman had been murdered, and looking at it steadily she tried to guess the secret it hid, and in some way surprise it as it slept.

What forced her to this she could not have said. . . . Had she considered the situation she would have realized that to loiter there at all was to ask for undesired attention, and to awaken suspicion. There might be someone watching from behind the closed *volets*, it was well within the bounds of probability. The thought froze her. She turned away, and walked a few steps along the street, strongly under the impression that she was being watched, and then she drifted back again.

Yet there was nothing unusual anywhere in the street. The taxi stood before the door of the hotel. People went and came, and the shadowy prostitutes slipped out in their secret, discreet way, offering their invitation. She saw them all exactly where they had been, and the taxi, it didn't move off, only the two policemen had gone.

"It's nonsense," she said to herself. "I'm going silly. Is it likely a policeman would sit there every night, spying through the shutters watching people pass. I'm crazy."

Though she reassured herself, she was not really satisfied, and she turned towards the market. She thought that the noise and life there would drive out the uneasy sense of something wrong. Once there, with the shouting and traffic close round her, she felt better. There was plenty to distract her eyes and mind. She wandered along watching everything, and her attention fixed itself on a butcher's stall, piled up with carcasses of animals.

A heavy, sick smell hung in the air, and further down a booth where sausages and bacon were sold was crowded with purchasers, who bought platefuls for a few coppers. Every one near her was eating, and an old woman ladled out soup from a wooden bowl and handed it around to a waiting queue. She had to walk carefully to avoid treading upon horrible leavings, thrown to the ground, and went on more quickly to where the carriers were unloading high carts piled with cabbages. Further on again there were mountains of lettuce and other vegetables, and a sweet smell of wet earth, fresh and clean, came in with the carts. It made her think of small hedged gardens, and herbaceous borders where mint and thyme grew, and she remembered a Sunday when she had gone to see her little boy in the country, and held him on his legs to walk in his stumbling, child's way along a garden path.

In those days her life had been almost happy. There was some meaning in it. She had deprived herself to save enough to pay for him with those people, to buy him toys, the funny little clothes he wore, his tiny shirts, and cakes and sweets for him. God alone knew how much love she had poured out into it all. And then he died. . . . They had buried him away there in the country, and Léontine, breathing in the smell from the vegetable carts, remembered as she stood there the desolation of the small open trench where they had hidden away her son. All the old anguish and ill flooded over her, all her pain. She recalled the day of the cheap little funeral as though it had happened yesterday. It had been so lonely, for no one knew them in that strange place. This was exactly the same smell of freshly-turned earth. . . . She was blind with tears.

She had never forgotten anything of it all, or the garden scents, sweet with fragrance. It was queer. It was for her alone, that night, in such a strange place, so unlikely and so tragic, only for her, that it returned.

Everything pointed towards that. Her rupture with Lampieur, her cowardice when she was face to face with him, her dreams and her crowding fears. . . . Could she deny it? She had always had such dreadful trouble. She had prepared the way for worse things to come, was so used to it that she almost felt a kind of wretched satisfaction in her own wretchedness. There should be some limit to what one was asked to bear. It always seemed as though she had reached breaking point, and that made her hope that fate might relent, and strengthened her belief that there might be consolation somewhere.

A man behind shouted at her, and she started.

"What's wrong with you?" he asked. He was drunk, and felt kindly towards her. He imagined she might listen to him and come home with him.

"It's as you like yourself, of course," he said, with drunken dignity.

She was already far away from him and was out of the market, and taking the Rue Turbigo, she hurried back to the neighborhood of the bakery. Her unhappiness drove her back to Lampieur. He only counted with her, and she forgave him everything. She was drawn to him. In the taxi shelter that blocked half the street, she heard the clock strike half-past two. She hurried on and turned the corner into the Rue Saint-Denis. As she reached the air hole where the light streamed up, she saw, a little further on, a man standing motionless watching the entrance to a house. It was Lampieur.

## CHAPTER 18

"What? It's you again?" he said.

"You must get out of this at once." She spoke in a changed voice.

"Why?" He didn't seem to understand what she said, but for all that he followed her away along the pavement past the gloomy facade.

"You," he said heavily, as he walked. "You have come back, you're back. . . ."

"What were you doing there?" she asked.

"That's my own lookout," he said with a sort of pleasure in saying it. "I'm a free man, I suppose, and have a right to go where I like, haven't I?"

"Come," she entreated. "Quickly." She dragged him into a neighboring street, tugging him by the arm, telling him that she had something very important to say to him.

He looked at her questioningly and threw back his head, but he went with her, and so she gained her point.

When they were in the next street Lampieur stopped dead.

"Now," he 'said, "what's all this about? What's this story?"

"Someone is spying," she said in a whisper.

"Someone?"

"Yes, hidden behind the shutters. . . ."

He started and drew back. "Are you sure of that?" he asked.

Awakening himself from a heavy stupor, his features took on an expression of sudden agony which moved her indescribably and made her long to help him.

"They're after me," he said, staring at her. "That's sure. Well, here I am."

"Wouldn't it be better to leave the quarter? . . ."

"What are you saying?"

"I think," she replied humbly, "that it might be better to clear off. Don't you see that?"

"I see," he answered. "Where could I go to?"

"Away from here."

"No," —the word was dragged out of him,— "I don't want to. . . . It would be the same thing, anyhow. You think that would make any odds. . . ."

"Still. . . ."

"No," he said persistently. "For you to come and tell me that there was some one behind the shutters, means that you saw them there. If you did, why didn't you tell me?"

"It was only a minute or two back," she explained. "I stopped . . ."

"In front of that house?"

"Yes," she admitted.

He swayed on his legs and fixed her with his eyes, quite silent and breathing hard.

"We can't stop here like this," she said frantically, and drew close to him again.

"Behind which shutters ?" he asked.

"The first story."

"Swine." He spat out the word.

He made up his mind suddenly, and stopped swaying about to look more closely at Léontine. She turned from him, hiding from the searching look he held her with, and clung to him.

"I'm not lying," she said. "Oh, come away. Listen to me. The man inside the house may have gone off to give information. He may have guessed. . . ."

"Guessed what?" Lampieur asked.

"That it was you."

He gave a heavy shudder, and again she begged him to come away. She clung to his arms, dragged at him with all her strength, but all to no purpose. He threw her off, walked away a few quick paces and then staggered against the wall. She ran to him, clasping him.

"Go to hell," he said. "Clear out. I shall go home by myself."

"Lean on me," she said.

"You?" He spoke contemptuously.

"I will come too."

Léontine supporting him, they got back to the Rue Saint-Denis. She did not know what they were doing, neither did he, but he kept on repeating, "I'll go. . . . I'll go. . . ."

Where did he intend to go? She did not dare to ask in case it should anger him, and yet she dreaded that out of some fatal desire to haunt the place of the crime, he meant to return there again. If this was his intention, what would become of him? She was convinced that there was someone inside the house, and that it was already too late to escape the unseen watcher. Without intending to, she had awakened suspicion first of all, herself, and she reproached herself wildly, now that it was too late. The one thing left was flight. Why was Lampieur so determined not to give in to the necessity? She couldn't understand that. . . . On the other hand, it was impossible for her to forsake him without trying again to help him in his dense bewilderment of mind. He seemed to have become absolutely astray in his wits, and he repeated the same words over and over again, shivering.

"It's all right," she tried to calm him.

"Keep steady."

"Go on," he told her, and again he began to mutter quite unintelligible phrases, looking madly round him, and taken by fierce shuddering, as his teeth chattered.

"We'd better go back," Léontine advised him, but he made a sign to silence her.

They stood perfectly still for a little in front of each other, saying nothing, Lampieur unable to control the fits of ague shaking which tore him. The streets were gradually awaking and the little shops opened drowsily. People began to pass, and the girls coming out of the market went by in twos and threes, going home to bed. There was no use accosting any of the men at that hour of the morning. They were trooping off like animals on the way to their stalls, with reins loose and the harness hanging. Léontine remembered when she had been one of them, and watched them enviously. She remembered the special feeling of that morning hour, and how it lighted up the vague, wandering intoxication. . . . Now nothing of all that remained except bitter regret. Was it her fault? It was Lampieur's fault rather than hers. If it had not been for him and the fascination he had exercised over her mind and body, she would never have thought of changing her life, or that there was any need to lift herself up from it and redeem it. What had given her that crazy notion? She ceased to try to think, and bowed before her shattering distress.

"Come along," she said hopelessly, "aren't we ever coming away?"

Lampieur took her arm and, holding on to her, turned to climb the hill, making a long detour to avoid passing the house or being seen by the man who, as they both believed, waited for them inside.

## CHAPTER 19

From that time onwards the hidden man became their sole preoccupation. They thought him everywhere, and the fear he inspired in them was unbearable. Lampieur never slept. All day long in his room he lay there wide awake between the sheets, his eyes fixed on the handle of the door. At times he believed he saw it move as though it were going to turn, and he shut his eyes.

A strange feeling as though he were covered by a shroud surged over him, and he reminded himself that the door was double-locked, so that he might dare to look at it again. This knowledge reassured him very little. He was terror-struck. The sweat poured from him, and Léontine, who slept no better than he, caught his horror from him and lay there still and frozen to the soul.

As nothing happened by the end of several days, Lampieur began to work again. She went into the cellar with him, for at first she had not the courage to go out into the street as she used to, or to sit in the bar, waiting for Lampieur. Between them and the bar stood the awful house. When she did go out, she straggled past the market and found her old friends again. It heartened her up to be with them, and they gathered in at the cabaret belonging to Fouasse, where she stood them drinks. They talked to her and asked her questions, and she chattered feverishly, trying to forget. It was a relief and a change from the horror-stricken life she led with Lampieur. Then Lampieur came in and sat down at the table where she was with the other girls, who slid away and left them alone.

"See you later," she called after them. Monsieur Fouasse came to the table.

"Well?" he asked Lampieur who was surprised to see him so friendly after his long absence from the place. "Well, what's up?" He shrugged his shoulders. "Don't let us quarrel, Monsieur François."

"That's all right," Lampieur said sullenly.

Léontine sitting between them, as they seemed to find nothing further to say to each other, smiled mechanically, and fiddled with her glass.

Lampieur's hidden trouble weighed too heavily, he made her suffer too much. . . . Then, he was so strange that she could not pierce into the darkness of his incoherent wanderings. Instead of feeling safer as the days went on and being thankful for his deliverance from the pit from which he had escaped, he imagined fresh traps laid for him. He opened his heart to Léontine, driven by some urgent need to speak. He talked of the murder, and hinted so clearly at his own act that his feverish talking threw her into a crisis of new alarm.

It was useless to try and prevent him from this insane longing he had to talk. It obsessed him. She remembered the days when he guarded his black secret closely and would not have spoken of it to any living soul. She did not want to know. The closer he came to telling her all the details, the more determinedly she withdrew, with active hostility, but he did not care. It was as though he felt her to be an ally, intimate and part of himself. Had she not been attracted from the first by the thought of the murder? He only saw that, and now his egotism made her necessary to him, it gave him a hideous satisfaction to uncover his memories.

## CHAPTER 20

She was not mistaken. Her sense of the situation as it stood between her and Lampieur was clear and unerring, as she foresaw the ultimate result of living close to him. When he had ill-treated her, she had forgiven him, and had lent herself to him to be used against the forces that flogged him on. Now it was different. His cowardice was too evident. She pretended so well that it was not possible to suspect her secret disgust. What difference did it make any longer that he accused himself of the murder? She had always known he had done it. Did he imagine it would soften her? He ought to have thought of that before, it was too late now As for finding any morbid interest or excitement in the revelations he made, she had none. There had been too much of it.

The regret she had felt when she saw the string of prostitutes going back from the market worked in her. Once she had gone along the street without a care. What had become of all those good times of hers, and were they never to come back? She sighed as she remembered them. At least they had—except for her métier of the night hours—complete freedom.

She compared her own wasted existence with that of those girls. What a contrast there was. She felt cheated. She must have been out of her mind to agree to live as she did with Lampieur. All she ever thought of was the bad mistake it had been, and she set her mind on the one longing to get out of the prison that held her, and go back as quickly as was possible to the old, queer, wayward life.

She changed under the persistency of her ruling thought, and it did not escape Lampieur's watchfulness.

"What's up with you?" he asked, but she said nothing. She had taken steady refuge in silence, and only bent her head.

"There is something," he said.

She refused to sit in the cellar while he worked at night, and his suspicions began to stir. She was often with those girls and might make confidences. They chattered and whispered and were well able to draw her on to talking too much. They would surprise her into saying things. Was he at the mercy of a gossiping talebearer? He became reserved again. What madness had urged him to confide in her? His own folly had been stupendous, for if they ever guessed from Léontine all he had told her, she would not deny it. Even if she were to deny it. . . . He fell deep into a tragic perplexity of mind. His last hope was slipping away, and he saw the end.

Anyone else would have gone away. He could not make up his mind to that. The day following the crime had decided all his conduct, and still decided it. It was less a reason than cowardice, a kind of inconsequent weakness. The apprehension of being arrested paralyzed his will and made him submissive. It worked directly on his mind. He could not trick himself or dispute the truth, and yet why should such a thought keep on tempting him in spite of himself? Just to chance everything, and in one moment redeem the menace of his destiny. A feeling stronger than self-protection drove him. He gave up the effort to resist, and it brought him a strange reaction, made him drunk with exaltation.

Lampieur realized this in a thousand different ways which all of them concentrated on Léontine. In his frenzy he clung to her. He wanted to believe that she did not talk . . . he wanted her to be his faithful accomplice. . . . Was that too much to ask? At times he lost confidence, and told himself he would oblige Léontine to explain what she was thinking of behind her silence and whether she really was hostile to him.

She had no reason to speak of what she knew. She had partially recovered her liberty and made no secret of it. . . . This partial liberty was not enough for her.

"Exactly," he said, reproaching her. "When you're finished with me, you'll clear off."

"It's like that," she said.

He bent his back, leaning forward. "And if I don't like it?"

Léontine gave a shrill little laugh.

"Don't imagine you can say or do what you like, because I put up with your going off as you do."

She repeated her laugh.

"Stop it," he shouted. "If you're going round with those girls and take them for your pattern, you'll get on all right."

"Oh," she jeered at him, "the girls I go round with. . . ."

Lampieur looked at her. "I know what I'm talking about. I've seen it all, ever since you went back to Fouasse. That's the truth."

In leaving the bar that very morning they had quarreled noisily in the street, on the way to their room. Léontine had dragged behind, she did not want to go back.

"You go ahead," he ordered her.

She faced him with an insolent look, laughing at him as he walked towards her.

"I'm off," she shouted to him, and running away up the street, she left him without any explanation, or even giving him time to recover from his dismay.

## CHAPTER 21

All the rest of the day his feelings went beyond anything he could express. He was deeply humiliated, and he nursed his misery in the room where everything reminded him of her. Their strange intimacy, their mutual distress, the habit they had fallen into of suffering with and through one another. He was alone in the face of his sorrow, and he felt that soon it would overwhelm him and get beyond his power to endure any more.

What could he do? How could he carry it, weak as he was, to the end where revelation awaited him? He was lost in advance. . . . While Léontine had been there to bear it all with him, how little or how much of it fell upon her only affected him indirectly. Once she was no longer there to protect him, he trembled to think that everything was discovered, and he waited crouching before his advancing doom, without resistance. Up to that point, in spite of the violence of the blows he suffered from his wretched fate, none of them had reached the wound itself; it was now no longer protected, but gaped nakedly, defenseless against further attack. His craven abasement at the mere thought crushed him to earth. The more he continued to think, the more he realized that there was no way of escape.

Léontine was no longer there for him to wreak his irritation upon her and bully her. This much became clear, and he shivered, catching his arms round his body. He had not thought of that before, why was it ?

He called to her . . . without her, what would become of him? Already he was growing aware of a little of all she had done to help him, and he steadied himself against the wave of fresh pain. But how . . . and to what extent? He felt that the time approached, and the thought of Léontine protected him again as he drew back like a man who had seen a bottomless pit open beneath his very feet, and is drawn towards it, in spite of his own will. . . .

As his last stronghold fell, Lampieur realized his loneliness. He drank in a bitterness that he had not known before, and yet he understood that something deep within him had need of this searching and awful anguish before it could live. He awoke with a dull amazement to a sense of an inward existence which, since his crime, he had lost hold of completely.

What did this strange transformation actually mean? It pointed steadily towards that hidden end. Lampieur was like a man who in some mortal danger sees the whole of his past life, and in one second is given some disconcerting proof of the truth. . . .

He longed to go and find Léontine and bring her back, but that was not possible. She had made this strange new wave of feeling rise around him because she had left him, and he must endure the consequence of her loss. He resigned himself to that. Gradually he saw the reason for his isolation from her, and he accused himself with a rough sincerity.

Under the influence of this mood, Lampieur came step by step to trace back the course of events to the murder itself. Since then, he thought, he had not awakened completely from his trance or penetrated its full horror. This time he remembered the incentive which had forced him on. He had been in exactly the same state of isolation as he now found himself in, and it weighed on him. He was burdened by the same lack of purpose, the same self-contempt and dejection. . . . He remembered it all. Out of all his life, that special period was the strangest. He had dragged through the monotonous days and nights with their dull futility. What was the use of going on? He had no vices to amuse himself with, he was dull and had nothing to look forward to. Each evening when he left his room he knew that he would do exactly the same things at the same hour the next evening, moving in a tiny circle that ended with a drink at the cabaret kept by Fouasse. He was horribly discouraged by the thought. The people he saw were all without the smallest interest for him. He watched them, nevertheless, looked at them as if they were mechanical toys with no real life of their own. He leaned on the zinc counter in company with them, smoked, went and came . . . was that life?

Beneath his heavy exterior he hid a perpetual nervousness. It mixed into everything and was like an intermittent flame that flared up, so that he did not know how to control it. But it gave Lampieur a feeling about himself for which there was no ostensible justification, and yet which offered him a kind of solace.

It dawned on him that he was more different to the others than it was possible to believe, but he did believe it and saw at the same time that the less he thought about this the better. He felt a sneaking satisfaction in the knowledge. Then under the stress of circumstances, the gratification of it had diminished, and he grew uneasy as to what effect it might have on him.

Everything had disgusted him. He had remained for weeks together in a bewildered state of mind, and he tormented himself and waited for some circumstance to present itself to give him a chance to test his own defiance, or at least not to see it crumble and decay under his eyes. He had always lacked audacity, and he wondered anxiously what opportunity would ever come to him to make his experiment with himself.

Then one morning Madame Courte came into his bakery and began to complain about having to keep all that money in the house, at each quarter, when the rents were paid in.

Though he tried to keep himself quiet, he could not. He did not sleep. He hung about the cabarets until night and looked around him insolently. In the end he had been more than half drunk. . . .

His manner and bearing struck them with surprise. He nearly betrayed himself under his incautious exaltation, but he did not realize it. He was not actually responsible for what he did and he was thinking of the concierge. He saw that the decisive moment of his life had come, and that he was ready for it. It was like a reprieve coming to him when he had given up all hope. Like a great deliverance. . . . He steeled himself and made ready. . . . The wine he had drunk had intoxicated him far less than the desire that burned in him. He understood that two or three days later.

Some time remained for him to prepare his plan, between the October and the January quarter. He ripened his project and arranged how to carry it out. In the morning he left the bakery, and sometimes, instead of going up the street, he turned down and looked along the corridor where he intended to steal on quiet feet.

The concierge's lodge was at the far end to the right, and looked out on the courtyard. One evening when she had been away, he inspected it. There was no door at the back, but windows on every side lighted it as well as the tiled floor of the lodge. From across the tiled floor you could see into the room itself, and he went and looked for a long time. He came away fully reassured, as a curtain, which she drew every night, hung along the length of the wall.

Towards the end of December Lampieur was ready. His plan was quite clear in his mind, and he knew the name of a tenant of one of the flats which he could shout to her, coming in after midnight, so as not to disturb her and make her get up to discover who it was who had come in. Here he was met by a difficulty. To get into the lodge, it was not only necessary to have a key, but to push back the bolt which would certainly be drawn across. It would be difficult to do this without making any noise. That bolt was his worst obstacle, and on the evening of the murder Lampieur went in after dark and loosened the screws, leaving them so that a sharp push would make the hasp ineffectual to keep him out.

Once that was done, he went back to his own room, and made a parcel of a suit of clothes, a pair of gloves and light shoes, and having done this, he began to work again. He was absolutely calm. He put on the suit, having brushed it carefully, and cleaned off every trace of flour from himself. As the clock struck the quarter hour after midnight he went out, and it was not until he came back that the smallest sense of having taken any risk came over him, or the least foreshadowing of the dangers that threatened on every hand.

"The old woman. . . ." He started and fell back.

Sitting there in his bed, completely dressed, he saw the poor old creature towards whom he had been quite pitiless. . . . He thought he heard her. He could feel the throbbing of her throat between his hands, it palpitated and swelled as he gripped it. It was sickening. He let go his grip very slowly, half drowned in the hallucination of his own memory, and tried to move away again as the body of the woman he had murdered fell heavily on the covering of the bed.

He could not have told where he was, and he sprang from his bed, the terror of his vision following him. She was everywhere he looked, and he was hurrying from side to side of his room like a wild animal in a cage. Nothing forced him to stay there, that much still remained, and the idea that he could go away if he wished, reassured him a little, only it was all so unnatural. Was he really free if he was thus driven to the extent of seeing the old concierge and trying to run from her? She did not go away. She stayed there, following him. . . .

In the end he ceased to resist the vile hallucination, and tried to become accustomed to her. His whole look changed and he felt a trembling of his soul. Nothing now was left which could add to the evil, it flooded him with disgust towards himself, until the two horrors merged into one as they rent him.

He was forced to look at the bed, tumbled and disheveled, with the body thrown across it, lying quite still in the tragic immobility of death. Then the body on the bed expanded. Under its weight the sheets tore into a ragged hole. Lampieur could not escape and was forced to endure the foul contact, and struggle against it. The more wildly he fought it off, the more the sense of being caught in the cavity in the bed strengthened. The more the body drove in upon Lampieur, the more helplessly he cried out, and repeated, "Why is this? Why?"

There was no answer to his question. He could not answer it himself. He was dragged through the vilest infamy. A moving filthiness, the stench and the madness of which terrified him. Lampieur sank helplessly, he had no hope left. He saw himself utterly abandoned, and in the face of his unspeakable punishment he was powerless.

## CHAPTER 22

He stayed in his room until evening, but no calm came to him.

At seven o'clock he locked his door and went out. He was ghastly white and trembled so violently that the most casual passerby must have noticed it. He cared nothing whether they did or not. In the street he brushed against walls and shop fronts, his eyes fixed in a dazed way on the lights. They fascinated him, and gave him a sense of drunkenness. More than once he stopped before a shop window, his eyes glistening, and he appeared so strange, and his look full of such extraordinary significance, that people who passed turned to glance back at him.

Every one he passed turned to look at him, but he saw no one, and expected nothing from anyone.

His old instinct took him to the cabaret. He recognized it, and remembered the bar and the windows, but he did not go in, he turned to the left and, still attracting the attention of the people in the street, found himself in the Rue Saint-Denis.

The road was narrow and ran obliquely between grey housefronts. Here and there lights showed in the windows, standing out vividly above the pavement and the rows of trees. He looked at them savagely, keeping onwards, but he felt himself beaten. . . .

Where was he going? Force of habit thrust him on, but it was not with any idea of returning to his work that he plodded forward.

Something further was waiting in there, and he went on with a queer kind of anxiety, the unanswered question making him hasten his steps.

During the short distance that divided him from the bakery, the question attacked him so fiercely that he had to stop and stand in the gutter to prevent himself from falling. Why was he suffering so dreadfully? The vision he had called up burst out upon him again and drove him abjectly. He could not go through any more or live through the vile repulsion it inspired. His legs felt weak, his eyes swam, he was choking and would have rather died a hundred times than go on living in the state of anguish that oppressed him. He was gripped by a suffocating rage of fear that perhaps he was again to be forced on towards a still more secret and abominable horror.

At last, he accused himself as the real author of his own distress, and he despaired, even when he fell a prey to this inrush of remorse, of any hope to avert his fate. He was sorry. A torrent of disgust surged over him and his conscience revolted. He had done it. How could he be absolved? He would have gone on his knees to the grave of the poor old woman, and knelt there and cried, if, in exchange, she would let him rest. His abasement was complete. In his incoherent way, Lampieur clung to the smallest comfort. Was he really responsible? He remembered that he had been honest, and repeated that it was not his own fault that he was a murderer. How could he tell that it would ever happen like that ?

Was he asking so much, after all? One minute's rest . . . one minute, one second even. Wouldn't they give him that? Why not? Was it that they couldn't hear him entreating? He knelt down and beat his breast and implored for mercy. Could they repulse him? Hadn't he endured enough? Was he to go through more? He consented in advance. . . . What? Was that not yet enough? What did they want of him? If they told him, he would obey, and ask nothing.

A voice commanded him to get up, an inward voice which made his nerves shiver again.

He went on with bent head, and going in at the door which he pushed open violently, walked down the steps to the basement.

A workman whom he did not know was in the cellar. "Is it you I was sent to replace?" he asked.

"It is," Lampieur said. Going to the wall and scraping at it, he dragged out a heavy stone. Taking the money which had been hidden under it, he put it in his pocket without replying to the astonished man who followed him as far as the door.

It did not take more than a few minutes for Lampieur to get back to the house he had passed earlier in the night. He looked at the facade for a long time, then at the door, went back again and crossed the road and returned. There was a kind of consolation in giving way to the memories that absorbed him as he stood there, dragging them forth from himself, one by one.

"That's it," he repeated half aloud.

The door stood open. He had shut it behind him. He remembered the dry sound of the cordon, and the automatic click that replied to his ring. Then he had gone in; he walked along the corridor and got to the far end. . . . What memories! They pictured it for him exactly as it had been, and showed him the interior of the dreadful, narrow passage. They made the moments which preceded his crime come to life again, and surrounded him with such vivid power that he expected to see the door yawn open again to allow him to come out. . . . He drew off and went across the street to the opposite side. He was talking to himself and could not keep quiet as he moved up and down, gesticulating with his hands.

In front of such a place it was impossible for him to escape notice. People looked out and stood together talking. Lampieur took no heed of them, but continued his pacing. They went away, but in the windows faces looked down, watching him. . . . What was the man doing there? Was he drunk? He wandered up and down, looked about him, stopped and then walked on again. What did he mean by it? They didn't dare to say what they really believed, but they were angry with him.

"Look here," one of them shouted, "you get out of this."

He lifted his head. . . . He could see faces looking down at him and others in the street watching him strangely.

"They'll fetch the police," a woman screamed after him.

"The police," Lampieur repeated. "The police." He burst into a stupid laugh and, shrugging his shoulders, went on.

Other windows opened and the neighbors began to shout remarks across. His folly showed itself in an instant and he began to run, turning up the first street that led into the Boulevard de Sebastopol, and walked down it with a rapid stride.

## CHAPTER 23

It was hardly eleven o'clock when Lampieur went along the Boulevard Sebastopol, and it took him less than five minutes, in spite of his detour, to come back to the Rue Saint-Denis at the top of the Square des Innocents. Once there, he breathed a sigh of relief, and he walked more slowly. He went round the square, the thought of Léontine replacing his former obsession little by little. She drove away the old woman, and his torment subsided. It was here, by the dark entrances to grimy little hotels, that she and those of her kind plied their trade, and hung about in dark passages or under archways.

He looked about him and spoke to one or two women, passed them after a word, and retraced his steps, waiting without moving from where he was, in case chance might send across his way the woman he wanted to see.

It seemed quite possible that she might come to one of these hotels. He saw Madame Berthe walk in with a man, and a little later Renée. . . . Madame Berthe came out again. She went off and came back with another passerby, and Lampieur slid away so that she should not recognize him. Everywhere in this quarter these vague places of resort opened late, and girls standing under the street lamps spoke to him or called out after him, offering to go with him. It humiliated him bitterly. He imagined Léontine employed in this base traffic, and a jealous irritation against her made her suddenly hateful.

"Come over here," a woman suddenly cried out to him from the opposite footpath.

He went on, pretending he had not heard, and taking a cigarette from his pocket, he leaned against the wall and began to smoke with bent head. What could he hope for from Léontine? What could he say to her? She disgusted him. She was one of these tragic prostitutes who steal along the road offering themselves for hire to the first comer. There was no difference. He was nauseated by the thought, and he saw that he was mistaken in not going away and trying to begin his life away from her and alone.

He could feel the money in his pocket, and the touch of his fingers against the banknotes recalled the awful moments he had suffered a little while back.

He began to prowl round the square again, and his roughness reinforced him as he thought once more of Léontine. If she was ready to come, he would take her with him. She had suggested it herself. He ought to hurry. . . . The money hidden in his pocket would help, but Léontine must come too. Without her he was helpless. The day he had passed had upset him, and he could not face another like it. It was beyond his powers, and he would rather have given up everything than go through it all again.

But she did not come. He threw away his cigarette and lighted a fresh one. There was a bar near the square. He stood watching it, and he went on looking into each cabaret in the streets around. He must have gone into at least a dozen bistros, and he searched the meanest of them for her. As his hopes vanished, he blamed her more and more for having chosen to leave him as she had.

What did it matter that she was a girl like the others who crossed his wandering path, dishonored as they were? He felt no shame at the thought and forgot his righteous denunciation of her. He was no longer either jealous or angry. What did it matter? He found excuses for her. What if she had gone back to the streets? Compared to him, she was blameless.

Yet he could not find her anywhere. He went further and further, waiting by the entrances to hotels, near bistros, and other women whom he did not want came after him. He avoided them silently. After a time some of them began to recognize him and left him unmolested. They let him go on his fantastic search. He didn't interest them any more, and he noted their indifference, feeling that, after all, he mattered nothing to any one. He kept on steadily, going in now and then and drinking at the counter of a bar, until it was after midnight, and the shops began to reopen before he was aware of it.

During the night he had seen so many people gathered inside the cabarets drinking, and wondered what brought them there? Why did they look at him as he drank his rum? He suspected them of knowing where Léontine was. Then he drank another rum, and another. He went on to the next bar convinced that they all knew, but would not tell him, where Léontine was.

His feeling that she was common property increased in strength, and he made no attempt to hide the fact. He even dwelt on the idea with a shamed pleasure.

No abasement was too low. But had these men no mercy? He looked at them. They were work people from the market, and Léontine had probably counted them among her clients.

The thought of the girl and the sight of all these men humiliated him afresh; it destroyed something that mattered in him, it was overmuch to have to bear. When he found her, he thought, and took her away, he would really have paid the full price for the right to begin afresh. Disgust, abject humiliation . . . he had tasted it all. . . . His cowardice made her indispensable, and slowly he accepted everything, as a strange necessity in life or death, from which there is no escape.

## CHAPTER 24

All night Lampieur abased himself inwardly until in the end it gave him a dull satisfaction. He loafed from one to another of the wine shops and bars along the market and became deliberately drunk. The prospect of meeting Léontine, having suffered such cruel tests as he had for her sake, lighted up his darkness, and he felt quite certain that they would meet. A sense of conviction grew upon him that they would. The belief was part of his drunkenness, and it seemed all perfectly natural, as it encouraged and supported him.

What further test remained for him before he could meet the girl and persuade her to come away with him? He didn't know. It was a matter which had to be settled between his own conscience and a kind of tardy justice. Whether this confused and still distant fate would be moved to pity or remain inflexible, he could not tell. Lampieur resigned himself. He submitted in advance to the share of suffering which had been allotted to him in this unseen calculation, and his thoughts took him backwards and forwards over his mournful path, reassuring him and making him hope that this hidden fate was keeping count of it all.

In the end Léontine became the embodiment of his fate for him. She was the symbol of his expiation and deliverance. Above all, the hope that she could help him encouraged him in his idea that he would leave the quarter where the police were tracking him. She would back him up and see him through.

All this time it was getting late and dawn was beginning to show. Still Léontine did not come, and her absence made it impossible for him to do anything except wait for her.

In the streets he knocked against passersby and made his way with difficulty. People struck at him, they pushed him out of their path. He did not mind . . . he drew back and made room for them to go by and then went on again in his hesitating way, keeping outside the crowds who were gathered around the high vegetable carts, busy unloading them.

In going onward he went from one pavement to another, and because he was drunk, they appeared to him to move from side to side, and he made quick, foolish detours to right and left. All that wouldn't prevent his meeting Léontine and telling her that he had found her . . . found her.

The longing to see her increased into the idée fixe of a drunken man. That was all he thought of. In spite of his wanderings, he believed that he was being guided directly towards Léontine, and was more than ever sure of this when, having lost himself hopelessly, he recognized the little bar in the neighborhood of the bakery where he went every morning.

She had always waited for him there.

He went in and looked around the shabby clientele and the poor people who clustered round the two or three tables, and steadying himself drunkenly, he avoided upsetting the objects in his path. She was sitting at a small table with a cup of coffee in front of her.

"It's me," he said. He pulled up a chair and sat down, yawning. "What will you drink?" he asked her.

"Where have you come from?" Léontine said in a voice of astonishment.

"Down there . . . the market. . . ."

She got up, and called the garçon.

"I've paid," she said. "Let's come away. It's quieter outside."

He followed her patiently out into the street. Having found her at last did not surprise him. It was what he had expected would happen. Only, once he was in the street, he began to be less satisfied, and thought of the people who had threatened to send for the police. They might have done it.

"Hurry . . . hurry," Léontine said, pulling him by the sleeve; and lowering her voice, she went on: "We can't go back to the bakery."

"I thought of that," he answered, speaking in a whisper. "They've warned the police. . . . That's it."

She turned round quickly.

"I know all about it," he went on. "I know."

He hurried as well as he could, obeying her, and as they went on side by side, he spoke confidentially:

"I've got the money. . . . You understand what I'm talking of? Then all we need do is to take a room in an hotel until night. You know these hotels? I've a lot to say."

"What about?" she asked, still guiding him as she held his arm.

"A lot to say . . . and about this money."

"I don't know any hotel," she said wildly. "I can't stop. I can't. I can't stay here with you."

"What?"

"I only came out with you to give you warning," she said wretchedly. "To tell you to clear out of here, and never come back. Leave me where I am. Clear off alone, you're safer that way, and there's still time."

"What are you talking of?" he stormed. "Alone? I'm not going alone."

"Then you're mad."

"I'll not go alone."

Daylight caught the tall housefronts and the steep roofs, lighting them and touching them with color. Everything was startlingly clear. Shops, houses, entrances to yards and stables stood defined in the thin brilliant sunlight. The heaps of filth in the street, the splashes of mud on the walls, obscene scribbles in chalk on doorways, everything that was caught into the clean cool light stood out, branded on the slow mind of Lampieur. A moment of awful lucidity came to him.

"They're after me," he said. "They'll catch me."

"Clear out," she implored him.

"If you'll come."

"Go, go." She was in an agony.

He shook his head and spoke in a drunken voice again. "I did think," he said plaintively, "that you'd have come. I thought you'd stick to me."

"I can't," she answered.

"Well, so much the worse for me. . . ."

He looked gloomily out before him, but he went on with her step by step.

Where was she going to? He didn't care and it didn't much matter. She represented his sole hope, and he only knew that he must not leave her for a single moment. Nothing else was of the smallest importance to him. He thought that he could persuade her, soften her, make her pity his loneliness. She was kindly. There was a great gentleness in the girl. She would agree to come away with him after a bit. Why had she appeared to defend herself against him? He couldn't believe she meant it. There was always something about her that he had never quite understood. . . . He wasn't drunk now, he was sure of that. . . .

He was able to walk steadily and he knew the look of the street, and the way she was going, while he tried to make out what her plans were.

Suddenly she stopped dead.

"There they are," she said.

He saw two or three men in plain clothes and round hats come out of a bistro and walk towards them.

"Don't stand still," he said. "We must walk past them as if there was nothing wrong."

"It's them," she said breathlessly. "I saw them before, last night in the bar. . . . They know your name. They asked Fouasse why you hadn't been in."

"Go on," he said. "Keep on the inside of the path. They won't notice me if I'm on the other side of you. We must talk, and take no notice of them."

"I'm frightened," Léontine said chokingly.

He thrust his hands deep in his pockets. He noted that they were trembling, and it made him savage with himself.

"You shouldn't have made all this fuss about my plan . . . we wouldn't have been here. . . . God, if they don't catch me now, it will be luck."

"I hadn't a dog's chance." She shivered.

"Go on," he commanded her.

They went forward several steps, watching the detectives carefully, with a dreadful fear upon them. The closer they came, the less hope there seemed of escaping the hard vigilance of the men.

Lampieur kept close to the wall, a bent, heavy figure. He shook and his pallor was ghastly. He pulled down the peak of his cap to hide the terror that looked out of his eyes.

"They'll know me," Léontine said. "They'll be sure to know me. . ."

He drew a long sighing breath.

"Look out," he said. "It's when we pass them. . . ."

"The swine." She spoke with a catch in her breath.

The police agents were some yards off, walking quietly between the rows of shops as though they were not specially interested in anything. Shopkeepers were pulling up the iron *volets* with a shattering noise. A little servant with an empty milk can was going with it to the creamery, and others were hurrying along carrying bread and string bags full of provisions, or with early editions of the papers.

"Look out. Go carefully," Lampieur said between his teeth.

The police agents did not seem to have noticed them. They were walking in the middle of the pavement, looking to right and left with searching glances that saw everything.

"Ah!" Lampieur whispered, "they're moving back for the cab to pass. . .

A night cab was coming back to the stables, and as it lumbered along the detectives were obliged to make room for it to go by across the footpath to the open doors of the hostelry. Hidden behind it, Lampieur and Léontine hurried on. They both believed that already the moment of mortal danger was past, when Lampieur felt a hand laid on his shoulder.

"What's this for?" he stammered.

Léontine called to him.

"You're wanted too," a voice said. "Don't make a row."

Lampieur let them put the handcuffs on his wrist without offering any resistance, and as they shoved him roughly on in front of them he did not dare to look at Léontine, who walked behind him crying quietly.

## The Tragic Self: An Afterword
## to Francis Carco's *L'Homme traqué*

This edition features Francis Carco's 1922 tale of murder and madness, *L'Homme traqué*, in Emile Hope's translation, first published in 1923 by Jonathan Cape in London. The following year, an American edition translated by Alex Jorand was published by Thomas Seltzer in New York, under the title *The Hounded Man*.[8]

While "l'homme traqué" literally means a man who is *tracked*, a "hunted man" would be a more common form of expression in English. Therefore Jorand's "hounded man" remains close to the original while adding a subtle nuance: a fugitive who's relentlessly pursued and thrown into a state of turmoil. But once we enter deeper into the tale, we see that Hope's decision to christen it *The Noose of Sin* displays acute discernment.

Though much of the drama occurs outside, on the street, the story structure resembles that of a classic "crucible" form. That is, the characters are trapped in the confined "space" of the underworld circuit near Les Halles, where they're forced to undergo their respective transformations.[9] Hope's evocation of a noose comes into play as the police incrementally close in on the main protagonists – drawing round them tighter

---

[8] A quick glance at the two versions is sufficient to show that Hope's rendering – although long out of print and very difficult to obtain – is by far the superior one.

[9] A legendary Parisian marketplace, Les Halles is also portrayed in many other French novels, including Emile Zola's *Le Ventre de Paris* (The Belly of Paris; 1873).

and tighter – with the implication that the final constriction will lead to prison and death.

As with most of Carco's noir novels, we're privy here to a turn-of-the-century demimonde: a tenebrous realm occupied by those who have lost their luck – or never had any to begin with. As Carco informs us at the very beginning (when describing their hangout, at a cabaret): "Everyone who went there was or had been unlucky. Hatless prostitutes with slovenly clothes and dirty hands trooped in at night, to warm themselves by the stove."

Frequented by the local riffraff, this hooker haven represents one of several overlapping crucibles from which the women can only dream of escaping. A few blocks away we encounter another key crucible: a subterranean, dungeon-like bakery occupied by the chief protagonist, Lampieur, who spends his evenings stationed beside his oven. An antisocial misanthrope brimming with spite, one evening he forces himself upon the helpless Léontine, who finds herself trapped within this hellish enclosure from which there is no escape.

Although it's uncommon, the surname "Lampieur" does exist; but one wonders if Carco employs it as a form of wordplay. *Lampe* + *peur* = lamp + fear. Thus, a "fear of enlightenment." Perfectly suitable for an underground man of such abject darkness, who's chary to illuminate even the most superficial of his foibles. (He's also referred to as "Monsieur François," in a sly nod to the author as doppelgänger; for "Monsieur Francis" was Carco's nickname.)

One is tempted to compare Lampieur to the baker in Raymond Carver's widely acclaimed story, "A Small, Good Thing." There we encounter an exemplary character whose loaves of freshly baked bread symbolize sympathetic offerings of nourishing emotional warmth and heartfelt empathy. But in Carco's netherworld, baker Lampieur offers only psychopathic domination and toxicity. The timid (but at times unwittingly courageous) Léontine – a prostitute whose fatal submissiveness constellates her attraction to this unconscious opposite in the form of Lampieur – is slated to become his terrorized victim.

In many of Carco's novels, free will undergoes a massive eclipse, overshadowed by a residue of intractable psychological imprinting. In *The Noose of Sin*, troubling environmental factors form the deepest, most stubborn roots. Lampieur's arrest is preordained not because of miraculous police detection work but because he's long since lost his willpower and is unable to plot a course forward, into a more conscious, self-aware, enriching life. Overtaken by emotions and impulses that he can neither comprehend nor consciously integrate, he even lacks the wherewithal to plot an escape and flee. His mounting madness triggers such overtly psychotic behavior that only a fool in such a gossip-ridden French *quartier* would fail to connect the dots outlining Lampieur's guilt.

Though he's a heartless murderer, at times the reader feels sorry for Lampieur, because he's also a victim of his own inner turmoil and a casualty of the brutal manner in which he was raised. While the latter is merely hinted at, his gestures and utterances are symptomatic of a man whose soul was trampled upon at some early stage of development. The same is true for Léontine: they've each been tyrannized.

And so, for a time, they're compulsively drawn together as they mingle among the dregs of society, shunted off and pushed beyond the margin of "respectable" French life. They remain linked in so many ways, especially regarding their alternating dominant and submissive roles. (A favorite Carco theme.) Even the initial letter of their surnames is the same. But by the novel's end, via an unexpected role reversal, Léontine assumes the more dominant position and attempts to liberate herself from Lampieur's inexplicable magnetism and set off, in a new direction.

One reviewer regards *L'Homme traqué* as a "slighter" version of Dostoevsky's *Crime and Punishment*; but the drama is more than just a Gallicized rendition of a Raskolnikov type in Paris instead of Saint Petersburg. For one thing, unlike Raskolnikov, Lampieur doesn't plan to use the money stolen from his murder victim to fund a grand plan of personal betterment. Nor is the homicide a "test" of some abstract existential ideology. Instead, the heinous act stems from an obscure desire to shatter the predictable pattern of his otherwise dull, vacuous life.

Carco's storytelling often provides just a minimum of biographical detail – a handful of essential facts – from which we can then draw major, fundamental conclusions about the characters. For example, regarding the background of the two key figures: Léontine tells Lampieur that after she gave birth to a fatherless son, she was ejected from her home:

"It was because of him I cleared off. They didn't want me there. Father turned me out."

"And your mother?" he asked.

"Never had one that I remember. And you?"

"Oh, they're still there," he said in a grumbling voice. "The old people go on the same in the same way. They're still there," he repeated, his eyes looking at some inward picture the words recalled to him. And then she saw a sudden gleam pierce through the shadow of his memory and blaze out for a second, filling her with instinctive fear of him, as he burst into a dreadful laugh.

"What?" he asked. "Have I been jabbering?"

"I don't know what you mean," she said reluctantly, fearing to draw his anger towards her. "Don't you remember at all what you said?"

"I spoke of the old people," he said harshly. "When I do that it makes me think of myself. They were hard. . . . It's past and over now, all that time, and a good thing it is."

"Then don't think of it," she suggested.

"That's it." He spoke half to himself. "Yes, that's it; still, there are things one remembers."

"That's funny," she said blankly.

"Dirty things. . . ."

"That's the same for us all," she agreed.


Carco deftly links her tragic history to the present when he has Lampieur cast doubt upon Léontine's claim that the photo actually portrays her dead child:

"And that photo on the mantelpiece. . . . Look at it, of course that wasn't put there for me, of course not?

It's an old trick, that dead baby dodge. They sell them in the shops round here. . . ."

"Hold your tongue," she cried shrilly at him. "What right have you to say such things to me?"

The reader doesn't need to know anything more about Lampieur's ruthless upbringing. With these three words – "dead baby dodge" – the monster shaped in the distant past now steps forth, into the present.

While Lampieur is a morally blind protagonist, the timorous and ironically named Léontine ("Lioness") is a doomed hero. Despite multiple forces that conspire against her (her horrendous childhood upbringing, bereft of maternal support; her lifelong socioeconomic marginality; her compulsion to remain by her torturer's side; her naive self-sacrificing nature, which results in her arrest while attempting to rescue Lampieur), her heart remains remarkably pure, regardless of the sordid environs through which it's forced to transit. No matter how foredoomed or hapless, her valiant attempt to escape and to start life afresh buoys our hope and sustains our interest. That she fails only makes her tragedy that much more poignant.

A final word should be said about a third major "character" in *L'Homme traqué*, that being the spooky house that hosts the murder. But to fully appreciate its depiction we need to examine some of Carco's other work.

"Monsieur Francis" is remembered as a poet of meteorological effects (especially when portraying the shifting climatic phenomena of fog, rain, and wind),[10] but he's above all a painter of urban architecture and landscape, utilizing the medium of words. A Parisian flaneur par excellence, he harbored an extraordinary passion for the architectonic, sculptural beauty of the streets: in particular, the evocative imagery of serpentine perspectives, crumbling plaster walls, ominous outposts, ambling figures disappearing around a corner, or shuttered facades that portend ill-fated affairs.

No wonder that he was so powerfully drawn to the artistry of his friend Utrillo, who accomplished with pigment what Carco yearned to portray with his quill pen. Among the first authors to ever appreciate the artist's work, this is what Carco says about Utrillo in his memoir, *From Montmartre to the Latin Quarter*:

Recall the perspectives, deserted for the most part, of his Paris streets and of the suburbs. There shines upon the walls, upon the houses with closed shutters, upon the brown windows of bistros a fixed

---

[10] In Carco's work, moods and shifting psychological dynamics are often reflected in outer, physical surroundings. Consider this passage from *The Noose of Sin*: "Out in the street the lights fell crossways, and silhouettes of the passersby were thrown on the window of the bar for a moment as they went onwards. A mist dimmed the glass, traced by long lines of water where the drops trickled slowly down. The same wet fog dulled the one mirror of the establishment, in its brown frame. On the floor amid the cigarette ends and sawdust, little streams traced their way, and whenever the door opened an icy wind swept in, bearing on it the confused sounds of the street outside." Or this painterly image: "It was evening, and the skylight showed a square of pale pink sky, calm and delicate with the shadow of the sunset still reflected on the soft clouds. He looked at it, and then he turned to her."

light which comes from nowhere, except from those dream regions which no one dares talk about. And what anxiety there is, an anxiety that cannot be captured, what an ambiguous, fleeting, unattainable presence, what a piercing call! It seems that, at the precise minute when he could have helped us, the only human being alive in the world had just turned around the corner of those plaster houses and disappeared forever. Why has he not heard?

[…] you look at it, you approach it with curiosity, as if, from behind the shutters someone were watching you, and you act as if you had not seen him. But is one sure of anything? Isn't it rather that other self, which every man spends his life crushing down, who before this canvas awakes as if by enchantment? Those places are so familiar to that other self! He knows them. I mean to say, he recognizes them and the emotion that seizes him – at that moment – is one which only a few human beings can feel […][11]

Note these lines in particular: "You look at it, you approach it with curiosity, as if, from behind the shutters someone were watching you, and you act as if you had not seen him. But is one sure of anything?" How reminiscent of the ghastly, spectral house of *L'Homme traqué*, which Léontine believes to be inhabited by a

---

[11] An excerpt from Carco's homage to Utrillo's painting, *Champeau washhouse*. For the entire passage, see Francis Carco, *From Montmartre to the Latin Quarter. Edited with Annotations and an Introduction by Rob Couteau*, New York: Dominantstar, 2024, pp. 184-185. (Originally published as Francis Carco, *De Montmartre au Quartier Latin*, Paris: Albin-Michel, 1927.)

police spy, who peers at them voyeuristically from behind closed shutters.

But here, the similarity to Utrillo ends. For, upon the vibrant facades of the artist's colorful dwellings there glows a luminosity that can only emerge from "dream regions which no one dares talk about." The stunning enchantment catalyzed by this limpid radiance is such that the authentic self, which is otherwise crushed or suspended in limbo, is suddenly vitalized and re-awakened – sprouting into being, plantlike, under fulgent sunlight. Sight leads to ultimate insight, and "the emotion that seizes him" is a telltale sign; for "those places are so familiar to that other self! He knows them." What a magisterial description of how a great work of art may impact the viewer who knows how to open himself to its thrall!

Five years earlier, in depicting the house in *L'Homme traqué*, Carco utilized these same bold creative powers, but he inverted the style and mood. His word-painting of the house is Gothic and sinister. And, unlike his minutely detailed descriptions of Utrillo's mesmerizing streets – in which every particle of the image and every molecule of the pigment seems ready to lift off the canvas in a paroxysm of seizure – he instead focused his broad strokes upon the cheerless aspect of the residence that hosts the murder, which he imbues with a lugubrious, hideous reality. The building resonates with all the charm of a sinkhole; and, Gorgon-like, it paralyzes both Lampieur and Léontine, halting them in their tracks. Instead of rejuvenating light, the facade is engulfed in eerie gloom. The unredeemed blackness of Lampieur's soul is drawn to it, for it serves as the perfect "hook" upon which to hang his morbid psychological projections. The setting produces a similar effect upon the despondent Léontine, who was already overwhelmed by "a black abyss of limitless despair." This is how Carco describes the scene as viewed through her eyes, as she lingers there:

> It was just the same as all the other houses, shabby and dirty. The entrance with its brown door, which had never been left open since the night of the murder, attracted no special attention. By day it was possible to see the long corridor, the narrow walls and the worn steps of the staircase, the glass panes of the concierge's lodge. Léontine remembered these details, there was nothing distinctive in it anywhere. Only now that the door was closed, there was something funereal and mournful about the house. The shut *volets*, the heavy outline lent it a strange effect.
>
> She wondered that no one noticed it. . . . Lampieur had avoided having to pass it for a whole month, and she wondered if he too would find it horrible to look at. Several times as they had crossed the road to avoid it, she had known that he shivered with a kind of instinctive dread.
>
> No one else, except themselves, would know that the house appeared to be waiting for something. No one else would guess that, or think why she was frightened, because it only affected her and Lampieur, and took a definite shape to them, brooding with its unutterable power. It was not the first time Léontine had told herself this, but it disconcerted her and seemed to leap upon her afresh, loosing a host of vague presentiments. She gave way to them, standing before the house where the old woman had been

murdered, and looking at it steadily she tried to guess the secret it hid, and in some way surprise it as it slept.

The secret concerns not only the gristly details of the brutal slaying. Léontine is also hovering at the liminal threshold of the secret self. For both Léontine and Lampieur it will remain an unconscious, unrealized, inner potential that's been squashed and snuffed. Hope and anticipation are now replaced by apprehension and alarm: portents of a diabolical fate that cannot be evaded. Hence, *The Noose of Sin* illustrates how that which cannot be redeemed forms the basis of tragedy.

## Carco, Modigliani, and the *Blonde Nude with the Dropped Chemise* [12]

*Nu blond*. Later titled *Standing Nude*; *Blonde Nude with the Dropped Chemise*; and *La Môme Haricot Rouge*. Paris. 1917. Oil on canvas. 92 x 65 cm. (Ceroni catalogue raisonné N° 193.)

Paris is the City of Light, but it's also a spectral city of celebrated ghosts. Two that haunted me when I lived there during the late Eighties and the 1990s were Amedeo Modigliani and his friend Francis Carco, the great French raconteur who chronicled the lives of so many artists in his memoirs, which are themselves works of art.

---

[12] Originally published in the November – December 2024 issue of *New Art Examiner* (Cornwall, UK) in their *Speakeasy: Paris Memories* forum, featuring essays by Maria Balshaw, Director of the Tate; Sophie Kazin, professor at Falmouth Art School; and sculptor Elizabeth Ashe.

In *From Montmartre to the Latin Quarter* (1927), which I recently had the honor of publishing in a newly revised edition, Carco tells a bewitching tale of his devotion to Modi's work during a period when most French art dealers scoffed at his labors. At that time, Carco, just like Modigliani, was living a penurious existence, subsisting in a cheap garret.

One evening Modi's Polish dealer, Zborowski, invites Carco to his lair, to view an assortment of these unwanted creations, which lean against a wall. The room is lit only by a candle held in Zbo's hand, so the men must crouch to obtain a better view. Within moments Carco is overwhelmed by their powerful beauty, and despite his poverty he offers to buy one with his last remaining francs. Zbo responds: "To you, I won't sell ... I shall give it. Here ... I give it to you ... because you love it."

The gesture represents an act of profound empathy, but it was also a shrewd move. After hanging this magical image in his modest hovel, Carco can't help himself: he scrapes together his meager funds to acquire additional works. He writes of the "delight" he experienced each morning in his tiny *chambre*, "when I woke amongst those nudes with milky and orange flesh, under their blinking eyes and their magnificent forms! ... They were women I loved, and I felt alive beside them. And they were alive: their presence excited me."

Carco would go on to publish the first in-depth critical appraisal of Modi's work in the Swiss journal *L'Éventail,* in 1919. Scholar Kenneth Wayne writes: "Carco's was the only article devoted solely to

Modigliani during his lifetime ... this article is one of the purest, most sensitive, and insightful pieces of writing ever penned about the artist and his work by someone close to him." Though Carco brushed aside the importance of the article, it helped to build a firm foundation of recognition for the beleaguered artist, and it sparked important recognition from abroad.

We don't know which painting Zbo gifted to Carco, but research has led me to suspect that it was the *Nu blond*, also known as *Blonde Nude with the Dropped Chemise*. In any case, it was certainly one of Carco's favorites, and it's featured as a frontispiece in his book, *Le Nu Dans La Peinture Moderne* (1924). In that text, his love of the portrait is expressed in a moving tribute.

He compares the forms incarnated by Modi's vigorous, enlivening brush to the daubs of the academic painters who preceded him: "the cold, sandpapered nudes of the art academies ... bodies made of inflatable rubber, breasts stacked like tiered cakes, buttocks of trembling jelly." But now, instead, "A breath exhales from [Modigliani's] nudes, the very breath of life ... Where is the image in which the fervor of living is better incarnated?" In paying homage to *Nu blond* he can barely contain his joyful enthusiasm: the model's "most delicious flesh tones"

blend, knead with an adorable lightness to whip with mother-of-pearl and pink, rub with amber, fluff with blondness, this triumphant freshness that an exquisitely attenuated light of an April morning caresses more than it sculpts. Between the light and the skin, there is this impalpable velvety garment, this "frozen" translucent flower, but where the lighting plays with all its shimmering: all this mixed, melted, less painted than sprayed on the canvas.

This was a time when art critics – even those in the avant-garde – were not afraid to pay homage to beauty; and they did so while being fully aware that the notion transcends its classical limitations. For there is, after all, such a thing as a beautiful idea, even one that challenges the notion of beauty itself. In *Nu blond*, a beautiful idea fully blossoms.

When first absorbing a work of art, I like to wait and listen for a word or phrase that evokes its essence. Here, the term "tender fire" comes to mind. Perhaps it was kindled by the iridescent blush on the unknown model's cheeks; or the blazing ripple of her cadmium-orange hair; or the brilliant tints of peach-toned flesh that Modi so fervently applied with dappled brush-work to create perfect complements to the undulating blue hues of the background. All of which infuse the portrait with vibrant intensity. It's as if a freshly animated being has stripped away her persona – dropping it along with her chemise – to reveal herself, and an equally bold artist attempts to capture this transcendental radiance.

The gleaming reflections that hover in her pupils are the focal point: they arrest our fluttering gaze and challenge us – and the artist – to gaze back. The first thing that struck me about this perpetually modern masterpiece is the powerful presence radiating from those eyes. On the one hand, her regard is confrontational: a stare that asserts dominance and unwavering self-assurance. On the other hand, it's softly alluring and seductive. Following the fine curve of her nose down to her puckered lips, we encounter a further expression of this budding warmth; and when we gaze back at the riveting orbs, their mood seems to have shifted, now conveying an unreserved affection.

Carco auctioned off most of his art collection in 1925, but he held onto this exquisite composition until March 1939, when it was sold at auction to the dealer Jos Hessel for 250,000 FF. The "liquidation" of goods – and of human lives – was in the air. Just six months later, England and France would declare war on Germany.

Carco slipped into Switzerland as the Nazis swarmed across France, but he always carried the memory of this collection with him – along with Modi's specter – like an intimate souvenir.

Francis Carco in Agen, France

Maurice Utrillo, *La Rue de Venise*, 73 x 50 cm. Purchased by Josef Müller for 11,000 francs in Carco's 1925 auction, lot N° 87.

Carco with Père Frédé, inside the Lapin Agile.
Photo by Michel Brodsky.

**Maurice Utrillo, *Place du Tertre*, 1911, oil on cardboard mounted on cradled panel, 54.29 x 73.34 cm.**

*The City of Shadows: A Romance of Morocco. Edited with Annotations and an Afterword by Rob Couteau.*

*The Lost Cure. Edited with Annotations and an Introduction by Rob Couteau.* Afterword by John Locke

*Dark Refuge. Edited with Annotations and an Afterword by Rob Couteau.* Postscript by Christopher Sawyer-Lauçanno

**Francis Carco:**
*From Montmartre to the Latin Quarter.*
*Edited with Annotations and an Introduction by Rob Couteau.*
Afterword by Christopher Sawyer-Lauçanno

*The Noose of Sin.*
*Edited with Annotations and an Afterword by Rob Couteau.*

**Stanley J Marks:**
*Murder Most Foul! The Conspiracy That Murdered President Kennedy: Edited with an Introduction by Rob Couteau*

*Two Days of Infamy: November 22, 1963; September 28, 1964* Introduction by Rob Couteau

*Coup d'Etat! Three Murders That Changed the Course of History. President Kennedy, Reverend King, Senator R. F. Kennedy.* Introduction by Rob Couteau

*A Murder Most Foul! A Three-act Play about the JFK Assassination.* Introduction by Rob Couteau. Afterword by James DiEugenio